GEOR

MW00709485

THE BOY WHO LOVED TREES
(AND OTHER TALES)

Cover image by: Mindbomb Design
Book design by: SWATT Books Ltd

Printed in the United Kingdom
First Printing, 2020

ISBN: 978-1-8381875-0-7 (Paperback)
ISBN: 978-1-8381875-1-4 (eBook)

George R. Spooner
Southampton, SO18 6AX

CONTENTS

The Boy Who Loved Trees...5
Heavenly Deals..17
The Breakdown...20
Britannia's Last Stand...24
Poor Tom..29
The Amulet of Osiris...34
Black, Black Friday...40
The Return of the Piper...41
Angel of the Sea...48
00:28...52
Garbage Lake...54
The Red Leather Chair..60
The Faceless Ones..65
Watching for Badgers..70
Left on a Park Bench..78
Life's a Picnic...80
Pick a Pickled Pepper...82
Jennifer THX..87
The Power of Three, Chris' Story...................................89
The Power of Three, Elizabeth's Story...........................95
The Power of Three, Wayne's Story..............................103
Hunt The Piper...110
For the Love of Mother..116
What the Cat Saw..123
One in Four...132
The Roses of War..133
Playing Board Games with Uncle Frank.......................138
The Girl in My Mirror..144
Southampton to St Ives...152

The Symptom of the Universe **158**
The Three Musicians of Muhren **160**
Under the Jetty **165**
The Corner Shop Redemption **175**
Plastic Dolls on Lying Pages **182**
The Pranksters **184**
The Last Hag **196**
Dinner at the Millers' **200**
No More Heavenly Deals **209**

THE BOY WHO LOVED TREES

I've come back to my old home to say goodbye. "Big Oak Creek", once part of a prosperous lumber industry, now just ruins of what was. I think of my best friend, Will Johnson. I close my eyes and try to understand what happened one more time...

My ma and pa, Hank and Marie Mills, arrived in Big Oak in 1894. In the July of the following year I, Josh Mills, was their first, and the town's first, child.

Working conditions for the timber workers were hard and dangerous. It wasn't unusual for men to drown or to be hit by falling trees. Occasionally someone would lose a limb or worse to the saws. The workers would toil for 11 hours a day or more. Pay, depending on the generosity of the sawmill owner, was between $1.50 to $2.50 per day. Some of my earliest memories were of Pa coming home to our log cabin, eating in silence and then falling, fully clothed, into an unrousable slumber.

Despite my pa's best efforts, Ma still had to find a job to keep us clothed and fed. She worked at Henderson's colonial-style mansion, which was situated some two miles from Big Oak, near the sawmill on the banks of the Brazos. Ma worked there three nights a week doing chores.

While some of the lumber barons exploited their workforce by enforcing poor working conditions and even lower wages, Henderson was a more reasonable man. He took a paternal shine to Ma and paid her $1.75 for a three-hour shift, effectively earning more than

Pa, not that he was bothered. Sometimes Henderson would ask Ma to work during the day if he had guests. Ma felt obliged to help as he had been so kind to her but that left the problem of me. Fortunately, Ma had struck up a friendship with the lady next door who also had a son of my age. She was only too glad to look after me and her own child, who would become my best friend, Will.

***

The school in Big Oak Creek consisted of a single room attached to the church. It was here that Will and I had our first taste of education. We were only taught on Mondays and Fridays and only five other children attended the class with us, as the parents of Big Oak couldn't pay for a full-time tutor. This suited Will because while I adapted well to the discipline of school life, Will yearned to be outside.

"Will Johnson, please turn around and stop looking outside," was the regular cry of our teacher, Miss Bainbridge, whose qualities of patience and kindness were often tested by Will's apathy. In any case, two days at school meant three days of freedom. Even at six years old, Will and I still had chores to do, cleaning at home or going down to Old Tom's Store situated about half a mile away. There we would buy dried goods or chicken feed. Everyone in Big Oak seemed to keep chickens. If he was in a kindly mood, Old Tom would give the kids horehound candy. If not, he would tell us to "scoot", which we all did without question.

After chores and milk and biscuits, Will and I would meet behind our cabins. There we would play amongst the trees. Hide and go fetch, Rebs and Yanks. Many childish games.

Sometimes we would rest against the oak tree, just talking about anything that took our fancy. One day, exhausted by the recreation of Custer's Last Stand, our version of which had Custer victorious, we took up our position at the oak.

"Do you ever think how the trees got here, Josh?" said Will, dreamily.

"Hell no," I replied, looking around to make sure Ma hadn't heard me cussing.

"I do," he came back. "They just stand there in all the rain and sun and such. They never complain. They look good with leaves on and they look sad when the leaves fall."

"What the heck you talkin' about, Will?" I really didn't know where this talk was going.

"I dunno. They just make me feel safe, 'specially this old oak."

"Do you think that we could climb it?"

"Dunno. Seems pretty high to the first branch," Will said, and then added, "Do you think we should? It might get angry."

I laughed aloud. "Jeez, Will, it's just a big ol' dumb tree. Let's go, yeller belly!"

We spent the rest of the afternoon just trying to reach that first branch. We were laughing and falling and climbing again.

Nothing seemed to change much at Big Oak. Some families came and some went. The town never got any bigger, unlike Will and me. Now eight years old we could reach that first branch and beyond. Will was better than me at climbing. He was taller and skinnier and more eager to explore.

**

We were sitting in the oak one August day when we heard screaming and shouting coming from Will's place. We scrambled down the tree, jumped over the back fence and went into the kitchen.

I've never forgotten the image that confronted us. Will's pa was laid out on the kitchen table. His legs were hanging off one end, twitching ferociously. One man was holding him down at the belt, another doing the same at his chest. Will's pa was crying out and cussing, tears rolling down his stubbled face. A third man was there. Everything was happening so fast and yet so slow. I knew this man; He was Doc Williams.

"Get the fire goin', Maude," he shouted at Will's ma. She was staring at the table, not moving.

"Now!" roared Doc.

His tone snapped her out of her stupor and into action. My eyes went back to the doc. He was tightening something around Will's pa's arm. I looked further down and noticed that Will's pa was bleeding. A lot. Then, before I ran out, I saw that Will's pa was missing a hand.

Life changed for Will after the accident. His pa could no longer work at the sawmill. Mr Henderson made sure that his family wanted for nothing and let them stay in town. This was extremely kind of him as a great many of the lumber tycoons would have abandoned them to their own fate. My ma even let Will's ma have some of her hours at Henderson's Place. The trouble was Will's pa. He started drinking heavily. Then you could hear him shouting. "I'm a Goddam cripple livin' off damn charity. To Hell with all of you!"

Old Tom was told in no uncertain terms not to serve him any more liquor. This he did despite abuse from Will's pa. It didn't matter much. With the sales of hard liquor regulated by people who didn't want their workforce drunk, the moonshiners flourished. Some of these moonshiners were considered local heroes for providing folk with hooch. It wasn't hard to get. Will's pa became a regular customer.

***

Will stopped coming to school so often. When he did, he was usually wearing bruises to his face. He dismissed any questions with a curt "I just fell over," but even the dumbest kid knew what was going on. It was hard to keep your own business in a small town. I would always find Will in the trees when I wasn't doing my chores or at school. Sometimes he would go deeper into the woods, among the pines, but usually he could be found on a branch up the oak tree. He had become withdrawn. Gone was my friend who would run with me, shooting imaginary six-shooters at whatever enemy took our fancy. Now there was a quiet boy, hurting on the inside as much as the outside.

"Do you want to talk some, Will?" I tentatively asked one day, weeks after the accident.

"Ain't much to say," he mumbled back, looking away from me.

"Your pa hurtin' you, Will?"

"I said I ain't sayin' anthin'. Leave me be!"

I still saw him from time to time. He was still my best friend. Sometimes I would just sit with him in that big, old tree, not a word passing our lips. Now and again you could hear his pa calling. "Will Johnson, get your ass back here. I want to see you, Will!" Sometimes he would go back. I could hear his cries as that man beat him, and the cries of his ma as she tried to protect him. Now and again he would just stay in the tree until he thought his old man was sober enough that he could go back into the house.

***

One morning I looked out of my window and saw Will asleep in the oak. That huge tree seemed to be cradling him like a newborn, making sure he didn't fall. Life was sure hard for Will. I hoped it would become easier as the time passed.

Will's pa grew weaker with the hurtful effects of moonshine whiskey. Will got stronger. Although we were still boys at 12 years, Will could now put up some resistance to the beatings which, although they were fewer nowadays, were still ferocious. Even though Will no longer went to school, spending time doing chores and working at Old Tom's store on occasion, we still met by the old oak now and then. Will was now more open about what was occurring at home. He was becoming very concerned about his ma.

"It's like she's dyin' real slow, Josh," he told me one day.

"She looks really old and thin and pale. The old man picks on her more, what with me getting stronger and that one-armed bastard drinkin' himsel' to death.

I dunno what I'm goin' to do if she gets really hurt." I looked at him. Sadness clung tight to my guts as I watched orbs of tears rolling down Will's face unabated.

"You'll do the right thing by your Ma, Will," I said. "You'll be fine."

We sat in silence watching the uncaring sun disappear beneath the tree line. The call for supper came for both of us. Reluctantly, we parted.

I read for a while in my room after supper. The words passed my eyes without meaning. How could I help my friend? Ma and Pa had already told me not to get involved with the troubles next door. I had asked them why we couldn't interfere.

"Well," said Ma, "people's business is people's business. And anyhow, Josh, the Good Lord will look after his own. You mind your business."

But I couldn't accept this. I needed to help my best friend. My thoughts were knocked sideways by a fearful din. I looked out of my window and there was Will and his pa tussling in their backyard. I could also make out, by the light from the kitchen, Will's ma holding onto her husband's leg and being dragged along as he tried to grab Will with his good hand.

"Get off me, woman!" he shouted and flung the stump of his arm back, catching Will's ma flush on her nose. She cried with pain as her man approached her. "When I'm finished with this son of a bitch, I'm a comin' back for you."

The menace in his voice sent icicles down my back. He turned to Will. Will had not run away. He stood there facing this man who had become a devil.

His pa drew nearer. "You think you're man enough, boy. Let's see what you got."

As his pa took one step more, Will hit him and hit him hard with a log that he had found in the yard. His pa slumped to the ground.

"Run, Will!" I shouted. "For God's sake, run."

Will turned and ran. He hurdled the picket fence and rushed towards the oak. He climbed like the Dogs of Hell were close behind him. He finally settled on a branch a mighty way up. He looked into his backyard. His pa had disappeared. I could see him visibly slump, like an old man. I breathed a sigh of relief, perhaps his pa would respect him a little more and leave him be. Perhaps, hopefully, he's dying in the house. No luck. The backdoor crashed open and out stumbled the man himself. This time he was carrying something I couldn't quite see in the darkness. When he got to the bottom of the oak, he pointed the object up towards Will. In his one hand, cradled into his ribs, was a shotgun.

"You come down here, Will, or I'll blast you out of that Goddamn tree!"

"Go to Hell, you drunkard!" Will cried back, the fear in his voice apparent to all who heard it.

His pa raised the shotgun up to his shoulder. I held my breath. Then, in the blink of an eye, Will's pa was raised up into the air. The gun flew off as he was flung around like a rabbit in the jaws of a large hound. I didn't have the best view from my room, but I am certain that something from the ground, like a very thick rope, had grabbed Will's pa's ankle. He was still screaming and cussing when the rope stopped as abruptly as it had started. There he was, suspended in mid-air by something that had come up from the earth. There wasn't a great deal of time for Will's pa to think about his ordeal, though.

An almighty crack pierced the night sky. A large branch from the oak pivoted from the trunk and hit Will's pa with terrible force. It struck him on the head so fiercely that his head assumed a strange angle to the rest of his body. The rope-like entity released its grip on his ankle and Will's pa fell to the ground with a nauseating thump. The rope then arrowed into the ground and was seen no more, its task complete. Will came down from the oak and stood over his pa. There was no sympathy from him as he spat on the still corpse. He then returned to the backyard to tend to his ma.

The sheriff from Kirbyville arrived late the next day. Will told him that his pa was drunk and when he tried to climb the tree he fell. The sheriff had no reason to disbelieve Will and, with the absence of any other witnesses or evidence, rode back satisfied to Kirbyville. I could have spoken out, but Will was my friend. I was still unsure of what it was that I had actually seen. Frank Johnson was buried soon after. Not many came to his wake.

To my delight Will came back to school. He had much to catch up on. Unlike the Will of old, he went about his studies with renewed vigour. He had been relieved of a mountainous burden. We carried on as if nothing had happened, playing amongst the trees and resting in the arms of the great oak, Will's saviour.

It was in the oak that Will spoke about his ma, not more than a month after his pa's demise.

"I thought that she would be happy, Josh, what with the old man gone. But she cries a lot of the time. Sometimes, at night, I hear her call out his name. I don't understand it at all."

"She's just grievin' for him, Will," I replied, as tactfully as I could. "They were together for a darn long time, you know."

"I suppose you're right," he said, unenthusiastically. "She'll be all right, I'll make sure of that."

***

Sadly, that wasn't the case. I was with Will when we entered his house after school one day. It was the first time I had been there since his pa's accident. I was still a little uneasy about the place. Looking at the kitchen table where he had been treated didn't help. I quickly followed Will, who was calling for his ma.

"She didn't say she was goin' out," he said with a hint of worry.

"Maybe she's in the yard, Will," I offered.

We made our way outside. His ma was still nowhere to be seen. We looked around as if she might suddenly appear out of the air. I turned to Will to discourage him from further searches and he was stood motionless, looking up towards the oak. I slowly followed his line of vision. "Oh my God," I said breathlessly. Hanging from a branch, swinging gently in the breeze of a glorious day, was Will's ma. She looked like somebody's abandoned doll, a doll who had given up on ever being loved or wanted again. A shoe had fallen off from one foot and was sitting on a pair of wooden steps situated just below the empty vessel that was once Will's ma.

"Ma! Ma!" screamed Will as he rushed towards the oak. "I don't believe it. Why, Ma, why?"

Will was hugging the tree as if it were now the only guardian he had. His loud sobs shook me out of my shock. I started to walk to my friend. I got to the picket fence and stepped over it. Looking up, I saw the strangest sight that anyone could ever witness. Will was melting into the trunk of the oak. He was sinking into that old grey/brown bark as if he were no longer solid, just water in a skin. By the time I got to him, Will had gone.

My thoughts were in a whirlpool but there was one thing that made sense. All the bad things that had occurred, the death of Will's parents, his disappearance, were all centred around that oak tree. I let out a roar and rushed home. The tree must die.

I found an axe in our front porch and headed back. As I raised the axe, it didn't occur to me that it would take years for a scrawny teenager like me to fell this beast. I was just so angry and confused as I swung the first blow. Before the blade made contact, I heard a voice, loud and clear.

"No, Josh, no!"

It was my friend's voice, but it was too late. The axe embedded itself in the thick torso.

I looked around. Had I imagined Will dissolving?

Another shout. "Josh, take the axe out. You're hurting me!"

I hadn't let go of the tool. I began to rock it back and forth to loosen it. After a short time, the axe came loose and I pulled it completely free. The open wound in the oak was not showing new white flesh as I had expected. Instead, a red trickle ran down in between the scales of the bark. It flowed almost to the base of the oak and then stopped.

I examined the blade of the axe and that too was showing red.

"Thanks, Josh and goodbye, my best friend," were the last words that I ever heard from Will.

***

Another piece of tumbleweed feels the force of my boot. I never told anyone of what I thought had happened to Will. It was said that after his ma died, he just took off. I believe, no, I know that he's in that oak tree. If I had told folk what I saw and heard, they would have locked me up for madness. I'm off to war now. To some goddam country in Europe that I've never heard of. It has been said that thousands of men have already died in the three years it's been going on. There is a good chance that I might not come back. If I did there is an even better chance that I will be dead. If that is so I have left one last request with Ma and Pa. I want to be buried at the foot of The Great Oak.

I might, just might, see my friend one last time.

HEAVENLY DEALS

This place has existed under numerous monikers. Zion, Canaan, Elysium, Arcadia. As the millennia pass slowly, less of humanity even believe it exists. Exists it does, although now I wish it would vanish and leave mankind to his or her own devices.

I look wearily down to a scene that I have witnessed on too many occasions. The marble tabletop is extravagantly inlaid with semi-precious jewels, pietra dura and mother of pearl. These elements intricately and beautifully portray planet Earth. My Earth. On each side of the table are three thrones. Behind each set of three is a larger throne. I can hardly bear to look at the figures sitting on one side. I didn't create them, but I did nothing as I saw them forged by man. War, Famine and Pestilence govern all that is hateful, harmful and heinous on that distant world. I can feel the confidence and smugness that exudes from these abhorrent entities. Sitting opposite are their foes, Peace, Plenty and Panacea. These are bodies that I have created. They once ruled supreme in the golden age of man. I hoped that they would be the preservation of mankind, but now they sit dejected, forlorn, almost defeated. The 'game' begins...

Each being has their own markers. These are strewn across the map to indicate where that entity is in residence. As this time, War has markers situated on Syria, The Ukraine, parts of Africa, for example. Pestilence follows the innocent victims of conflict. To refugee camps, spreading cholera, typhoid, whatever disease it feels fit to unleash. Famine is in those places too but is also littered around the globe in highly unlikely locations, such as North America and Britain - the so-called civilised countries.

Peace works in the Corridors of Power and amidst the instigators of war. It vies to inspire sense and mercy within the Dogs of War. Plenty attempts a similar strategy, persuading the bountiful to share with the needy. Panacea helps man not only in the research facilities on Earth but also in the field hospitals, the run-down convents, anywhere that Pestilence has struck. I do not need to declare which side of the table is winning.

They all squabble. War will place a marker on a different country where internal strife is making harmony very difficult. Peace will protest, to no avail, claiming that War has enough markers on the map to sate its desire for destruction. Then Peace will acquiesce and place markers near to all relevant parties, hoping that reason will prevail.

This pantomime will be played out until one of the evil entities declares a cessation to the debate. They command. They have done this for aeons. All parties rise, turn and vanish. That is not the end.

Sitting in the larger thrones and only materialising when their subjects have gone are Life and Death. They will discuss the outcome of the completed conference. They too will argue with very few concessions being made on either side. Life will protest vehemently against the number of fatalities and the amount of suffering heaped onto the shoulders of the human race. Death will counter with barely concealed conceit that the population of Earth is still expanding. Therefore, man can bear the losses brought down on him. At the conclusion of this secondary meeting, both parties turn and vanish. A status quo has been agreed.

I am left to look on. What I thought was a good idea has turned out to be a folly. I am powerless now except in the minds, hearts and faith of some men and women. I have one gift left. Unknown to War, Famine, Pestilence and Death, I keep it hidden in a box under the very table where they plot their evil machinations. It is a precious, essential commodity. I give a little at a time to those most in need.

Hope.

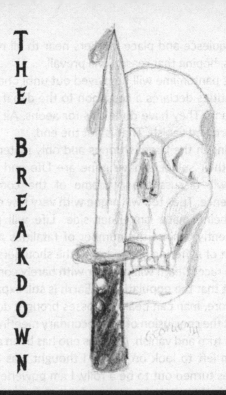

THE BREAKDOWN

I don't mind waiting. It's all part of the excitement. I've waited for weeks, months before an opportunity presents itself. I do copious amounts of research. Tonight, I am parked outside a late-night cafe southwest of Basingstoke near the A33. I only select A or B roads as my work needs privacy. This is the fifth night at this particular site. Two more nights and I'll find another location far away from here.

Almost midnight. A car pulls in. It parks quite a distance from the cafe. My racing heart pumps a little faster when the driver gets out. She is a female. And she is alone. I go up to the cafe and carefully peer through the window. The woman is looking at a menu. She then orders food. I'm in luck. I rush back to her car.

As I plunge the knife into the radiator, I become aroused. This is the appetiser before the main course of feeling the knife sink into soft, fresh skin. The hiss from the radiator is the dying breath. I lick my lips.

I follow the woman onto a dual carriageway of the A33. To my delight I see her brake lights come on. The car pulls over. The hazard lights are activated. To my left is a dense wooded area. Perfect. I pull in behind her car and turn on my own hazard lights. Before I get out, I put on a fluorescent jacket. It has ROADSIDE KNIGHT emblazoned on the back of the jacket and a smaller motif on the front. The woman is standing at her open bonnet. She is just a prize to me. I don't care what she looks like.

"Good evening. Need any help?" I say. I try hard to hide my excitement.

"Can you help?" she replies. "I know nothing about engines."

"It's your lucky night," I reply ironically. "Just get my tools."

I return with a toolbox full of appliances. I don't even know what most of them do. "I've been a mechanic for a long time. Hopefully we'll soon get you going."

"Oh, thank you," she gushes.

I look inside. I see my handiwork from earlier and smile. I spend a few moments touching parts of the engine in the pretence of mending it. I stand back and pull out a mobile phone that has never worked and try a number.

"Damn it!" I exclaim.

"What is it?" she replies.

"I need to contact the other guy on duty tonight. This repair is tricky. I'm going to need a second pair of hands. I haven't got the part I need for this. Only problem is my mobile is on the blink." I look at the woman. "Could I borrow yours, please? I'll pay for the call, obviously."

The woman hands me her phone. I walk away and make a call. When I've finished I put the phone in my pocket. "He's on a call at the moment. He'll get back to me shortly," I say.

"Can I have my phone back?" There is a note of panic in her voice. I think she is beginning to catch on.

"I'll just keep hold of it for a second. He said he wouldn't be long. Anyway, I'm sure that we'll fix your motor and get you going," I say. I am rapidly growing tired of this charade. Now I have her phone it is time for fun.

I breathe deeply a few times. Preparation for the kill. I reach into my toolbox. I grasp my favourite knife. An Italian stiletto. Sleek, gleaming and beautiful. The woman sees me caress the knife and lets out a shriek. She runs from the bonnet past the passenger side. Good. I like it when they run. She reaches the driver's door and gets in.

I'm walking around the car, taking my time. I hear the doors lock. Not a problem. I take a large spanner from the box and go to the driver side window. The woman is desperately trying to start the car. Fool.

"Let me in, little piggy, or I'll huff and puff and blow your door in," I say as the spanner crashes through the window. I reach in to open the door.

"Strike! Strike! Strike!" shouts the woman into her jacket. The ominous sound of sirens cuts through the night air. Someone pulls me from behind. I hardly notice the glass cuts on my arm as I am pushed to the ground. Handcuffs are placed on my wrists. I am pulled upright to face the woman. She shoves her police ID into my face.

"I've been waiting a long, long time for this, you bastard."

She doesn't even try to hide the contempt in her voice. I stare at her stoically.

"I am Detective Superintendent Carey Mullins. You are under arrest on suspicion of murder." As she cautions me, I hear an excited voice nearby.

"We've got him. The countryside killer. He's nicked."

As they lead me to a police van, I smile. I always liked that nickname. Nice ring to it. I notice head-lights approaching. I know who this is. The 'other mechanic' I contacted. He slows down, just slightly. We exchange friendly glances. He will be working alone from now on.

BRITANNIA'S LAST STAND

Britannia and her lion stood stoically on their plinth. Moss had showed them no mercy. Pigeons paid no respect. Rust had weakened her trident and shield. This Roman goddess looked out into the wide, green expanse. Giggling laughter filled her stone soul. The chattering of mothers made her belong. The creaking of chains, the whoosh of children travelling up and down. Round and round. She ached to smile. She prayed for the day to last forever. She dreaded the night.

As night fell, a group assembled in the play area. It was the ideal location for their nefarious activities. The nearest houses were too far for them to be heard. Minimal lighting provided camouflage. Trees and bushes provided hiding places, if needed. Britannia watched as the gang progressed. Marker pens and glue. Stolen alcohol. The introduction of drugs. Cigarettes, marijuana, cocaine then heroin. Sexual awakenings. Fornication among the group. Alpha-male fights. Fists. Bats. Knives. Swag exchanged to provide finance for their growing addictions.

The morning light brought the usual routine of the park warden clearing the debris before the arrival of mothers and children. He shook his head as he filled his bag. Empty cans. Used contraceptives. Syringes. Her face remained impassive. She wished she could weep. This was a new, evil world.

Nightfall. She could hear them approaching. Shouting and swearing. They passed by her on the way to the swings. Sometimes, one or two would urinate on her plinth. They would try to reach her feet and occasionally they succeeded. The evening commenced with a showing of stolen goods. They discussed and debated how much drugs the property would fetch. Then there would be drinking and waiting. Waiting for the dealer.

Britannia looked on one night as an unfamiliar face strolled innocently across the park. It wasn't long before the gang spotted him. The fool stood still as they approached. He said, "Good evening," to them.

After the resulting laughter, the mob stole everything from him. He pleaded with them to let him go home. Punches and kicks rained down upon him in savage fury. When they had finished, the young man was not recognisable from the innocent that had crossed the green minutes earlier. He whined through broken and missing teeth behind bloodied and swollen lips. He was warned not to report the attack, or his family would suffer at their hands. The gang then ran off to be engulfed by the night.

Watching the broken youth struggle across the grass, Britannia experienced a new sensation. A fire was lit deep in her stone chest. It raged through her body, up her arms and down her legs like a volcanic torrent. The fire filled her until it could no longer be contained. Britannia raised her trident and shield to the stars. She bellowed an unearthly cry that shattered the night. The victim wet himself before limping off into the trees, never to return to the park.

They came again the following evening. Carefree. Guilt-free. They took residence on the swings and frames. Cigarettes were lit. One of the gang pulled out some cans from a carrier bag. "Who fancies a brew?" shouted the youth, holding up the strong lager he had acquired earlier.

Her trident pierced some of the cans, spraying the sickly-sweet liquid over most of the gang. Wiping their faces, the group turned. There stood Britannia. She advanced closer to the startled mob. Some regained their composure and ran. Others screamed and bled as shield and trident cut them. The speed of the attack was frighteningly fast. Britannia moved gracefully among them, like a sublime ballerina. When she had finished, none of the remaining gang were left standing. She stepped through their broken bodies and returned to her plinth.

Britannia did not see the gang the next evening. She did not see them for several days. The next contact she had with them was when she felt the heavy blow of a sledgehammer. The impact broke her. Her top half toppled onto the path below. Small pieces of stone broke away as she hit the floor. Footsteps came towards her.

"I don't know what you are, bitch, but it's the end."

The gang member with the sledgehammer raised it high. His target was Britannia's head. The hammer began to fall. Before it reached its target, it was snatched away. The group looked. Standing with the sledgehammer in his immense jaws was Britannia's lion. She had taken care not to kill anyone during her attack a few nights ago. The lion held no such moral dilemma. He set about Britannia's attackers. Clawing, crushing and biting. The screams were louder this time. The blood flowed more freely. When he had finished, no-one was left alive.

The area around the plinth was cordoned off with blue police tape. In the glorious sun lay ten bodies. They had all suffered greatly. A pool of blood surrounded them. Parts of their bodies were strewn around the path. Hands. Arms. Legs. Scenes of crime officers collected evidence. Police officers interviewed passers-by. One detective passed close by to the plinth. He saw a large crack across the torso of the statue. As he walked around to the front, he noticed bits of stone missing from her face and parts of her robe. He then looked at the lion. It stood there impassively. The detective looked closer. The lion appeared to have blood around its mouth and claws. The officer looked again. He turned and walked away.

POOR TOM

OK, I've heard all your weird stories, but here's one that will make you lot choke on your beers. This happened quite a few years back when I was Detective Inspector out at a rural nick in Surrey. I don't expect any of you to remember the odd case of Thomas William Joyce.

Tom was an oddball character. Very quiet, unassuming, the sort of bloke that could leave a party and no-one would notice. A short geezer, about five foot five, bald on top, thick hair round the sides and glasses so dense that you'd need great eyesight to see through them. He also had a neat little Hitler 'tache, just to complete the picture. He lived in a tidy, little bungalow in a cul-de-sac, nice area, nice place. The neighbours said he was a very pleasant, polite guy, but nobody knew a lot about him. He kept himself to himself.

Tom worked for the same firm of accountants for 35 years. He had an unblemished record, never sick or late and never complained when others got promoted above him - which happened on quite a few occasions. Despite this, it was at work that life took an unexpected turn for Tom.

A secretary who had been there since the stone age retired. The firm hired a new girl, Betsy Dunlop. She was a real wildfire by all accounts. Big, brassy, blonde. A Barbara Windsor landlady type, if you know what I mean. Too much make-up, perfume and cleavage. Gave some of the old boys at the company palpitations, I can tell you. What nobody could understand was why she homed in on Tom. She would call him sweetie or darling and would leave her hand a bit too long on his arm or leg for his comfort. I doubt that Tom had ever had this kind of attention from a woman, never mind one 20 years his junior. A few months later, they decided to get married. Well, Betsy told him they were getting married. Life became very, very difficult for Poor Tom.

Betsy almost immediately quit her job and began living the life of Riley on Tom's bank account. She was often seen in new clothes, new shoes and even new cars. Now and then she would go on holiday alone. The Maldives, Seychelles, you know - down-market places like that. Well, Tom couldn't keep this up on his wages. He even used all his hard-earned savings to try and keep her satisfied. When that ran out, in desperation, he started to 'divert funds' from the wealthier clients at work. Not cut out for a life of crime, Tom started to crumble. He became a different bloke. Untidy, unshaven and even late. He also began snapping at colleagues over minor matters. It didn't take the management long to start asking questions. Tom crumpled like a cheap suit. Thirty thousand grand he'd tucked away to satisfy his missus. Sent shockwaves through the company, I can tell you. But they did the right thing by him. The losses were made up through company assets and Tom was 'encouraged' to resign rather than have the Old Bill get involved. It was a huge shock for Tom. A great chunk of his life had gone. In the end, as you'll see, it didn't matter much for Poor Tom.

With her lavish lifestyle gone and having to live on Tom's small pension fund, Betsy let herself go, big time. No more make-up or fancy clothes or getting her hair done. Instead she put on lots of weight and became very unpleasant. Neighbours could hear her screaming at Tom, calling him – in suitable Anglo-Saxon - a "failure", "wimp" and "useless". The bungalow started to suffer too. The once-ordered front garden became overgrown with weeds and uncut grass and the windows were in need of a good wash. Inside it wasn't any better. Tom had given up. Dust covered every surface. Newspapers and magazines littered the floor. The kitchen was full of empty take-away containers and dirty dishes.

In the bedroom, Tom's side was reasonably tidy, but Betsy's side was filthy. Empty boxes of chocolates, magazines, take-away cartons and dirty clothes that smelled like a mortuary on a hot summer's day when the aircon has broken down, were piled by her side of the bed. Life had become unbearable for Poor Tom.

One night when they were in bed, Tom quietly reading a paper, Betsy sucking the life out of hard centres and watching late night T.V., something happened. At some point Tom asked her if she would reach down among her pile of rubbish because he thought that he'd dropped his pen there. With the usual expletive, Betsy reached into the clothes and boxes and... SNAP! A bloody great bear trap bit into her arm just above her left elbow. It took a moment for her to realise, but when she did, the screaming and swearing started. Betsy then started hopping and prancing around the room, claret spurting everywhere.

Do you know what Tom did when this was going on? He laughed. He laughed loud and he laughed hard.

When the local plod turned up after several calls from the worried neighbours, forcing their way into the house, they found Tom in the bedroom still laughing. Big, old tears of laughter were falling from his eyes onto the body of the now-deceased Betsy.

Throughout the following investigation, whenever the bear trap was mentioned, Tom would laugh. Through it all he could barely keep the smirk from his face, but it was that particular moment that creased him up. He refused point-blank any legal help. When I had him medically examined, he was given the all-clear for interview. During the interview, which I conducted with D.S. Jack Carter, I found it difficult not to laugh. So did Jack.

Tom laughed when the charge was read out. He laughed when he was remanded in custody. He laughed when the judge sent him down for 25-to-life. As the court guards led him away, he was still laughing.

I'll tell you all something now. When I think of that odd little chap and imagine his horrible missus jumping around with that thing stuck on her arm, I can't help laughing myself.

Good old Tom.

THE AMULET OF OSIRIS

Peering through the window, I saw the same old tat. Rubbish that gives my profession a bad name. Badly taxidermied beasts. Old shell casings. Dead wasps. The tinkle of the bell affixed to the top of the shop door announced my arrival.

The air was hazy with restless dust and smelled dank and musty. A quick glance around reassured me that there is no competition here. A sharp glint caught my eye. In a corner cabinet an object glistened. My pulse raced as the item became clearer on my approach. A brooch. An elongated helmet adorned with ostrich feathers above an elegantly carved face. From the chin sprouted a long, rectangular beard. A pharaoh's beard. The brooch ends at the waistline, where the hands meet. One hand holds a crook, the other a flail. It was crafted in gold, emeralds and other precious materials. I was enchanted. I recognised the value of this brooch.

I eventually stood up. A figure at my side startled me.

"Exquisite, is it not?" A hunched figure dressed in a colonial-style safari suit stood there. Neatly cropped white hair crowned a tanned, weather-beaten face. The olive tone of his skin told of days of sun and sand. His voice hinted at faraway lands.

"Yes, it stands out among the other pieces," I replied.

The man held out a hand. "Ahmet Ra, at your command."

"Ra, the Sun God himself. Roger Squires, fellow antiquarian." Ra's hand was cold and bony. I withdrew mine quickly. "What can you tell me about it, Mr Ra?" I asked.

Ra unlocked the cabinet and passed me the brooch. "This is a very rare artefact. It represents the god Osiris. He was the Egyptian god of life and death. Of the afterlife and resurrection."

I *knew* this amulet was priceless. I did not need to be told its provenance by some back-street barrow boy. Despite my mounting joy, I had to remain calm.

Ra continued. "The brooch is said to have great powers. It has the mastery over -"

I interrupted him. "Yes, all very good. How much do you want for this little trinket?"

Ra snatched the brooch back. "It is not for sale. Not at any price. It is here to entice custom, which it has tonight."

"I doubt that it is worth very much, displayed among the rubbish that you're selling here. I'll give you a hundred quid for it," I said.

Ra walked over and opened the shop door. His eyes had narrowed to arrow slits. He was speaking through gritted teeth. "I would like you to leave now."

I gave the brooch a longing look as I left the shop. It was supposed to be mine.

The brooch played heavily on my mind over the next few days. That fool, Ra, didn't know what he had there. Lying in a cesspit was a priceless piece. Ownership would certainly raise my profile in the antiques world. I could charge a fee just for a viewing. This was an opportunity too good to miss.

***

I walked down the alleyway behind the terraced shops. Counting carefully, I found Ra's shop. The decrepit wooden fence and gate was in keeping with the rest of the premises. I put my torch under an arm while I fiddled with the padlock. I gave it one good pull and it came away with the surrounding wood. I stumbled backwards. The lid of a dustbin clattered onto the path. I froze, but nothing stirred. Shining my light around, I walked up to the rear door. It was solid mahogany, secured by three padlocked bolts and a dead-lock. "Bollocks!" I cursed. I sidled along from the door, hugging the solid brick wall. It made me feel safer. Fine pins pierced my skin and ripped along my face. I waved my arms in panic. A cat screeched and jumped down from the window ledge.

Then it was gone.

The attack took my breath away. I wiped my wounds. I could see a small amount of blood on my glove. Recovering my composure, I shone a light where the cat had been. I looked up to where an open window beckoned. Climbing on a dustbin, I pulled myself onto the window ledge. As I squeezed through, I lost my balance. The torch fell from my mouth and it clattered on the floor, its light vanishing. I fell after it. My fall was broken by a large, furry object. I caught sight of a cavernous mouth. Teeth were bared, ready to devour me. I yelled and started to fight. I punched. I kicked. This epic struggle lasted until I realised that I had been fighting a bear. A huge, stuffed bear.

I collapsed to the floor. My lungs gasped in the stale air. I was in a storeroom. Crooked shelves housed skulls, broken pieces of pottery, books in various states of decay all lit, along with a myriad of cobwebs, by the blue tint of the moon peering through the window. Recovered, I left this shit-hole for the shop.

The cabinet was unlocked. My trembling hands reached for the brooch. I felt a curious surge of energy through my body when I touched it. I did not have time to put the brooch in my pocket. The shop light went on. Ra was stood there, pointing a gun at me.

"You could not resist it, Squires, could you?" he snarled.

"Look, old chap," I stuttered. "I only wanted to have another peek at it. I wasn't going to take it."

"Liar!" shouted Ra. "You take me for a fool. I have every right to shoot you, claiming self-defence."

Sweat stung my eyes. "What do you say if we forget this little incident? Would five thousand pounds help? In cash?"

Ra smiled. Then he laughed. The gun dropped to his side. "You are an odious little man, Squires. If you desire the brooch so much, keep it."

I looked at him incredulously. "Thank you. You won't regret this. You'll get 30 percent of everything I make on the brooch." In my euphoria I had missed vital clues about this whole scenario. The brooch on display but not for sale. The ease of entry into the storeroom. Ra's sudden change of heart. He had organised this whole drama.

Ra sighed. "Before you go, I will warn you about the brooch's power."

Ra took off his cravat and the top of his silk pyjamas. His torso was covered in disfigurements. Discolouration. Pock marks. Craters. Severe ligature marks adorned his throat. He had been terribly mutilated.

"Good god man, what the hell happened to you?" I gasped.

"These scars you see are part of the price I have paid for eternity. For immortality. This gift is yours now. All you have to do is kill me. I am tired of this world. I saw the Pharaohs build their great pyramids in the time when I found this accursed amulet. I have lived through plagues and wars. I have loved many times and lost my loves to time. I was not honoured with children for fear that they too would be condemned. I beseech you, Squires, end my torture."

Ra handed me his pistol. I struggled hard not to raise the gun. I battled not to pull the trigger. The sound of the discharge echoed around the walls. Ra fell. His skin sloughed from his body. Internal organs turned to grey powder. This powder seeped through his skeleton onto the floor.

His bones then broke apart. They too turned to ash. There was nothing left of Ahmet Ra.

***

For what should it profit a man, if he shall gain the whole world, and lose his soul.

This quote defines my life. I feel no joy. No happiness. Wherever I travel, I see nothing but misery and suffering. Food tastes like ash in my mouth. Drink tastes like sour water.

My own collection of scars is quite formidable. I try to cut the thread. Despair leads me down into the valley of the shadow of death. Death does not want me. How long must I suffer? When will I find someone to whom I can pass the brooch? There must be another chosen one. Somewhere.

BLACK, BLACK FRIDAY

Beneath the surface
The beast is asleep
On the streets
Greed stirs
The beast opens an eager eye
On the journey
He stretches and smiles
He whispers sweet nothings
Of the treasures to come
At the entrance to Aladdin's cave
He has control
Open sesame!
The beast roars
He pulls the strings
"Go on
Grab what you do not need
Fight for what
You can do without
Feed my fire"

The beast yawns
It curls up inside
Beneath the surface
Of bruises and cuts
Of shame and guilt
A satisfied smile
Dresses his lips
"Until the next time"
Then he sleeps

THE RETURN OF THE PIPER

I remember sitting with my back to the open fire and looking at the expectant faces. The children were few in number as a vicious storm had left the village snow-bound and many of my pupils travelled from afar. It was story time. They had all huddled closer to the fire, faces reflecting the orange/yellow glow of the flames. The story was new to me. I had only found this book yesterday. It was decaying on a shelf in a storeroom that I was clearing. I opened to the first page. "Now children, this book is called the *Pied Piper of Hamelin*. I hope you all enjoy it."

***

Surrounded by the bones of the children that were borne of the treacherous folk of Hamelin, I have remained in this cave. I have mostly slept for the centuries that have passed, only awakening to hear my story when it is told, although it seems less and less these lonely days. I travel the Ether, the Spirit World, to stand unseen and feast upon the words of my tale. I remain a while until, like a frozen wind, I return to my prison, my sanctuary.

***

I finished the story and looked up at the children. I was not prepared for their reaction. Those who weren't crying, were visibly shaken and some had clung on to my assistant, Jenny, for protection and comfort. "Whatever's wrong, children?" I asked.

"I don't like The Piper, Miss. He's very scary."

"He's nasty, Miss. He took all those children away from their mummies and daddies."

"I'm frightened."

I had made a serious error of judgement. I had to rectify the situation.

"I know, children, after playtime we will all sit down and write letters to The Piper and tell him how naughty he is and that we want the children back. Is that a good idea?"

The children seemed pacified by this, to my relief.

***

I had been dismayed at the children's harsh words and my dismay turned to fury as I watched them scrawl on their parchment. "Nasty," "Horrid," "Evil," were just a few of the words that pierced me like a blade. Did they not listen to my tale? I was betrayed. Those fools at Hamelin had to pay and pay dearly for what they did. Now I have these urchins besmirching my name. I'll not let this rest. Along with their teacher they will also suffer for sullying my good name. They will fear The Piper.

***

That night I was sat at my typewriter composing an imaginary letter from The Piper. My desk was situated in the living room, facing curtains that struggled gamely to keep out the wind whistling through the gaps in the old French windows. Now and again the curtains would billow inwards, startling me as I saw my reflection in the glass, cameoed against the black of night. As I progressed, the curtains once more flew towards me; only this time, I did not catch my image but briefly saw the figure of a man. Uncertain of what I had actually witnessed, I stopped work and waited. Through the curtains came an abomination straight from the most terrible nightmare. A man, over six feet tall, stepped forward. He was wearing a torn and tattered green tunic and black and white striped trousers, ill-fitted to the spindly form of this creature. I could just about discern pipe-cleaner-thin legs which looked barely able to support this man and were completed by Turkish-style slippers.

The most hideous aspect of this apparition was his face. He had a very pallid complexion, one that had not seen the sun for some considerable time. His hair was wispy and fell about his shoulders like a white water-fall, which originated from a pronounced bald area on the crown of his head. A large hooked nose stood out from under eyes that were of the most piercing blue, a feature not diminished by the sunken sockets or the blackness that surrounded them. The creature smiled with thin, dark lips and revealed a mouth full of crooked, yellow tombstones between which poked a narrow, bluish tongue. I tried to scream for my husband who was sleeping upstairs but the figure held me paralyzed. Then, in two long strides, he was in front of me at the desk. He held up a bony, white hand and extended his index finger which he then shook close to my face as if to admonish me for some mysterious misdeed. Suddenly the curtains performed their usual trick. This phantom flew backwards through the now open doors, his gaze never leaving mine until the darkness claimed him as its own.

I tried to make sense of what I had seen. Did I imagine it? It was late and I had drunk at least two large glasses of wine with dinner. With uncertainty shrouding me like a cloak, I retired to bed, deciding not to relate this occurrence for fear that it would undermine my own standing in the community.

***

As I trudged through the snow the next morning, I was approached by Jenny's mother who informed me that Jenny was not well and would not be in class that day. This did not trouble me greatly as there were few children in school again. One or two more had managed to struggle in. I was more than capable of looking after this paltry number.

After register and morning prayers, I gathered the children around the fireplace which had been fed with fresh logs and was merrily crackling. I pulled out of my pocket the letter I had composed the night before, but as I opened the envelope there were several, startled whimpers from the children. They were all looking into a corner of the room, behind me.

I turned, slowly. Stood in that corner was the figure from the night before. He coughed as to clear his voice and a cloud of dust surged out of his mouth like a grey wave. He spoke with a rasping, parched voice, a voice that held all of us in deep thrall. "Who likes music?" he asked. "Do you all like to dance?"

The children all nodded in agreement, some of them even managed a smile.

"Well then let's put teacher in the corner and have some fun," said the man. With that I felt myself lifted off the floor and thrown into a far corner. Unable to move, I watched as the spectre produced a small musical pipe out of thin air and started to play. He jigged around the room. The children followed him, skipping and laughing, some holding hands. They passed the fire once, but on the second occasion the man stopped just after the fireplace. Still playing, he pointed with one skeletal hand towards the flames and the first child went towards them. I tried to scream, I tried to move, the Good Lord knows how I tried, but it was of no use. I watched as the first child stepped into the flames and, with a puff of smoke, disappeared. One by one the children all suffered the same fate.

Quite willingly, they were all taken by the flames leaving a small pile of ash as a reminder that they had once blessed this Earth. When the last child had gone, I was released from my invisible shackles. I rushed towards the demon, my fury outweighing any residual fear. My hands raised, ready to strike, but he had gone. I looked around but it was as if he had never been there.

When they found me, when they came to collect what was longer there, I was still by the fireplace. I screamed, not just because of the children but I had also suffered great burns to my arms where I had delved amongst the flames in the vain hope of finding something of comfort. I would never feel comfort again.

***

That was fun. Now back to my slumber; I've had quite a busy day. I'm not getting any younger and that has certainly tired me out.

***

They will never let me out of here. I'm not sure I ever want to leave, actually. I feel safe in here except when he visits. He will enter my dreams, sometimes my room and smile that cruel smile and show me the face of one of my beloved pupils. I will scream until they come and put me in profound sleep with their magic potions. Yes, I believe that I will stay here forever.

***

One last chore before I sleep. I'll just put my new little friends to bed. After all, I want their eternities to be comfortable.

ANGEL OF THE SEA

I came here to die. In this Eden. No better place. The sand feels like silk under my feet. There is no sound save the waves gently flowing in. They kiss the golden earth and return to their kin. A slight breeze momentarily troubles the tufts of grass that spring out randomly among the dunes. The rays of the sun journey through the virgin blue sky. The old fishing boat harmonises with the scene. It is neither ugly nor intrusive. It rests on the shore like a retired old man. It sees everything, and nothing.

Every shade, every sensation reminds me of her. Rachel. A love lost. When we were together, I wanted her so much it hurt when she wasn't with me. I changed my job to work near her office. Pictures of her covered my walls at home. I asked her to marry me so many times, but she turned me down. I had started to suffocate her, she told me. And that is what I did. She is buried deep in the sand. I would have brought her into the sea with me, but I could not bear the thought of her being eaten by the sea creatures.

I look down. I'd hardly noticed that I was in the water. Up to my waist now. The sea is tranquil and warm. It says to me, "Welcome. Join me forever." Chest high. No regrets. I'm crying. For Rachel. For the beauty of this day. For me. The gentle ripple of the surf strokes my crown. I take a deep breath of salt water. Not long now.

I open my eyes. I am staring into the corona of the sun. I feel the luxuriant sand. Is this death? I turn my head. Briny liquid seeps out of my mouth. I splutter and my gag reflex works overtime but I am alive. I am surprised to see the old boat. A figure looms over me. A blurry image. It crouches and looks into my eyes. I stare back. I become mesmerised. The eyes are black, as black as the coldness of space. As black as the soul of a sinner. Emotions invade my body and mind. Love. Joy. Euphoria. I am reborn. The figure moves away, back into the water. I plead with it not to go. It disappears.

I am a wreck. Everywhere I go I see my saviour's eyes. They penetrate my dreams. Ebony eyes that brought me feelings I never knew. I cannot recapture the passion I felt on the beach that day. I yearn for it. I ache for it.

The old boat is my home now. I wait with waning hope that she will return. I spend my days gazing out to the horizon, looking for a sign. Where are you, my love? My lust, my craving forces me back into the water. The waves try and push me back. The sand turns to treacle. I will not be swayed. Under the surface. Either she saves me again or I die, it doesn't matter in any case. My breath is about to give out, when I feel hands under my arms. They lift me above the water. I start to glide back to shore at a prodigious rate. In the shallows, I am dragged onto the shoreline. My rescuer is unaware that I am unaffected by this ordeal. I stand and face her. She struggles to return to the ocean. I hit out. She falls. She is mine.

I take her to the boat where I have manufactured a makeshift pool in the hull. I gently place her into the sea water and I look at all of her for the first time, real-ising that she is perfectly adapted to life underwater.

Her hands and feet are webbed, and fins run down her spine and limbs. She is svelte. I have made her a 'she' although there are no signs of reproductive organs. Is she the last of her race? Then I look at her face which is exotically bewitching. From the elegant shape of her head to the smoothness of her skin. The saucer shape of her eyes. I will soon be looking into them. I tremble with anticipation.

The rattling of her bonds alerts me. She is awake and desperately trying to free herself from the chained manacles which I have placed on her. Startled, she tries to dive beneath the water. It is not deep enough.

"Please," I say, "I am not going to hurt you. I want to be your friend. What is your name?"

Moving closer around the edge of the pool, I become aware of something I hadn't noticed before. My new companion has no mouth.

I take care of her as well as I can. I replace the water. I talk to her. I try to feed her fish. She turns them away and points to the sets of gills on the side of her head. How does she eat? I promise her that she will be free soon. I cannot let her go. It's those eyes. They are like a drug. I am becoming more and more dependent on them for emotional highs. The times between visits is getting shorter.

One night, an exquisite sound permeates the air. I sit up in bed to listen. The noise is tuneful yet melancholy. It might be the song of a whale. It is captivating. Then the longing hits me. A profound sadness. A deep darkness. I have the cure.

I go to her. She can ease my pain with one glance. I flick on the torch that provides miserable light in the hull. She stands in the pool. Her eyes are closed.

She seems to be concentrating. Then I hear the same doleful air. It rises in volume. The song is coming from her. Is she sending a message? The decibel level rises to unbearable. I enter her pool. I will not let anyone take her from me. I strike her into unconsciousness.

I think she is dying. Her skin was once a lustrous green. It has turned grey. Her fins stood proud on her back, legs and arms. Now considerable parts of them float away on the pool's surface. Most critical of all, her eyes no longer deliver the ecstasy I long for. I climb into the water and hold her. I must free her. I cannot let her go. As good battles evil in my mind, she dies.

I carry her home. I am crying. For her. For the lost feelings. For me. I slowly submerge under the surface. Through the misty water, I see several shapes. They approach me. They gently take her from my arms. They vanish. I take in the salt water. Not long now.

I am staring into the sun. I feel the sand beneath me. There is the old boat. A figure looms over me. It has the most gorgeous eyes. I cannot break my gaze. The realisation hits me like a truck. I am in a vicious circle of death and salvation. I cannot go from this beach as I am besotted by these angels of the sea. They are Rachel substitutes. I scream. Loud and long. The creature vanishes into the radiant blue.

00:28

00:28 Tired. Telly. Off. Scotch. Finished. Upstairs.
Undress. Wash. Teeth. Pill? No.
Sleep. Bed. Warm. Eyelids. Heavy.

00:47 Tap. Tap. Where? Window. Branch. Open.
Snap. Bed.

01:12 Chirrup. Chirrup. Insect. Cricket. Lights.
Search. Search. Corner. Found. Slipper.
Whack! Dead. Bed. Pill? No.

01:22 Screech. Squeal. Shriek. Outside. Cats. Dress.
Downstairs. Outside. Garden. Rain.
Shout. Cats. Bush. Stone. Throw. Smash!
Greenhouse. Damaged. Cats. Gone.

01:37 Inside. Dry. Undress. Bed. Pill? Later. Maybe.

01:59 Door. Open. Light. On. Wife. Drunk. Crash.
Wardrobe. Bang. Dresser. Eyes. Shut.
Pretend. Thump. Wife. Bed. Cover. Gone. Pill.
Two. Bed.

02:05 Awake. Wife. Snore. Nudge. Snore. Shove.
Swear. Pill.

02:32 Awake. Kicked. Punched. Pillow. Blanket.
Downstairs. Settee. Pill.

02:35 Tap. Drip.

02:37 Wind. Gates. Rattle.

02:39 Dustbin. Falls. Clang.

02:40 Owl. Screech.

02:42 Dog. Howls.

02:43 Enough.

02:44 Upstairs. Wife. Snore. "Quiet!" Grunt. "Quiet!"
       Swear.

02:45 Pillow. Wife. Smother. Struggle. Force.
       Struggle. Weak. Weaker. Finished.

02:47 Wife. Gone. Pill. Pill. Pill. Eyes. Closing. Pill.
       Pill. Heart. Slowing. Pill. Breathing. Shallow.
       Pill. Pill. Bliss. Eternal.

GARBAGE LAKE

I wandered down to Garbage Lake. The old bat had returned home, pissed as usual but without her precious Trixie. Apparently, something had leapt out of the water and cut its head off. I smiled. Mother had always loved that rat on steroids more than me. The bloody thing chewed my shoes. It crapped in my room. Now it was apparently sans head.

I didn't believe it. The coiffured cow probably had one G&T too many at the Horse and Cart and lost the mutt. It wasn't the first time I had to look for it. I didn't want to.

"I'll cut you out of my will, if you don't find her," was the usual threat. And the wrinkled witch did have a lot of money.

I went to the bench where she sat to feed the ducks and looked out over the lake. Garbage Lake. It used to be Gabbler's Pond. Many of us used to keep it in tidy order. Friends and neighbours working together. We cut back the foliage. We picked up the rubbish. The pond was our Eden.

People die. People move. Over time the volunteers became fewer. Those of us left did our best. It wasn't good enough.

My eyes welled. The smell reminded me of an old sewerage works I lived near as a child. There was an unsettling silence. No bird calls nor the croak of frogs. Not even a cricket. The bushes and trees and weeds threatened the pond from every direction. Cans, bottles, wrappers floated on her beauty. Beneath the stillness lay far worse. When levels went down during periods of hot weather, you could see her total shame. Shopping trollies, bicycles. Even mattresses. This was a slice of Hell that shouldn't be here. Nothing more I could do. Looking after the ungrateful Celia Grimes took all my time.

I turned away from the bench. Trixie would find her way home. And I couldn't give a shit if she didn't. One step away from the seat I saw a dark patch on the stony ground. Looking closer, the patch was wet. And red. Blood? A foot or two from this area was a tin. The label was missing, and it was holey with rust. The raised lid had blood dripping from its sharp edge.

***

"What do you mean, you couldn't find her?" screamed the ungrateful cow. "You get back out there and don't come back without her."

"Mother, I have searched for hours. She'll come back. She always does."

"If you want to sleep in this house again you will find her. I will cut you off from everything I have."

"Perhaps, if you come with me. Show me where you lost her."

"All right, you idiot. But don't forget what I said."

With the sun dying in the sky, we walked back down to Garbage Lake. We went to her bench. "Here," she said. "This is where it cut off my Trixie's head." She pointed to the dark patch by the bench.

"There's nothing here now, Mother. Are you sure that's what you saw? You do like a drink before-"

"Don't you bloody patronise me, you little sod!" The force of her voice made me step back. She carried on screaming at me. "If you cared anything at all about me you wouldn't let an old lady struggle out every day to walk a dog."

I could see people peering over the bushes on the far side of the pond.

"Mother, please. People are staring."

"Let them fucking stare. This is all your fault. If your father was alive, he'd give you a bloody good beat-"

She was stopped in mid-flow. A small object, expelled by the lake like a nuclear missile, hit her on the side of the head. She toppled over. The object rested by her. She looked at it. She started screaming.

I stared into Trixie's lifeless eyes. As much as I hated her, I did feel a slight tinge of sorrow. I picked up the howling harpy. "Come on, Mother. I'll get you home."

"Trixie! My precious puppy. You've killed her. You're a murderer!"

"Mother, listen. Please," I begged. She wouldn't listen. She kept hysterically howling.

"Murderer! Murderer!"

I could hear the people talking in hushed voices during lulls in Mother's screaming. She had turned a dangerous purple. The blow to the side of her jaw sent Mother sprawling to the ground. I hit her for her own sake, but I did enjoy it.

"He's hit her," shouted someone.

I looked up. The spectators to this farce were running up the path towards me. I looked down to the spread-eagled sow. She moaned on the ground. Her feet were resting in the water. I smiled. Just one kick and she would join the rest of the rubbish in the pond.

The water rippled. The surface then violently exploded. A large, rectangular object rose majestically from the filth. It then dropped on Mother. Her screams were muffled as the object dragged her into the water. Then all was calm.

"What have you done?" said the person standing next to me.

I stood there. In silence. In shock.

"Where's that woman you hit?"

I slowly turned to my interrogator, then I returned my gaze to the lake. The answer to the question was floating in the middle of the water. The mattress that had taken the old bat was slowly sinking into the stagnant waters. Impressed into the covering fabric of the object was the outline of Mother, including the image of her face contorted into an agonised scream. I wished the mattress luck and returned to the moment. I heard sirens.

As my face smashed into the dirt, warm, salty liquid ran from my shattered nose into my mouth. My arms were forced behind my back and I felt handcuffs being snapped on my wrists. I raised my head as far as I could. People were talking to policemen. They were shouting, pointing, even crying as they conveyed their accounts to the boys in blue. I was in deep trouble. I spat the blood from my mouth and whispered, pleaded with the lake for help. Please give up your secrets.

When the lake had taken Mother, I was in shock. What occurred next was clear and lucid. A tyre flew from the depths. It hit a young man in the face. His face exploded. Snot, blood and bone splattered into the air like a Jackson Pollock piece. He might have tried to scream but his lower jaw was hanging by bloody, visceral threads. A flock of hypodermic needles rained down. They were followed by cans, bottles, even the corpses of several bicycles.

Cowering under the assault the assembled multitude tried to protect themselves. Some started to run towards trees and bushes. They didn't get far. Blocking their way were assorted items that had emerged from the lake. Shopping trolleys, large petrol cans. My old friend the mattress was there with some new friends. The crowd found themselves being herded closer to the water's edge.

The aerial bombardment had ceased. There was a stand-off. The crowd stared in various states of awe. Many of them were hurt. Bottles had smashed on skulls. Syringes stuck out of eyes. Clothes were saturated with blood. Their gaolers surrounded them in a semi-circle. Every time someone stepped forward, they were butted back into the throng. No-one was going anywhere, unless the garbage decided otherwise.

The assorted junk started moving forward. Realising that they were about to get very wet, some people made a concerted effort to break through the cordon. The majority were knocked back into the filthy water. Two made it through and cheered in relief... Until a length of barbed wire slid at speed from the lake towards them. It grabbed the ankle of one escapee and dragged him back. On its return journey to the water, the wire wrapped itself around the other.

The escapees joined the rest of the mob in the lake. They thrashed violently in vain attempts to get out. Some were pushing down on the heads and shoulders of others. One man punched a woman in the face to get ahead in the race to the path. Nobody made it out.

The fading sun threw out its last rays onto the water. There were no signs of what had occurred. Just me. Standing there. Alone. The water parted. I walked freely into the path it had created. I stood on the bed of the lake. Surrounding me was all the garbage, interspersed with dead bodies. I smiled as the water lapped at my feet. I was still smiling when the cold lake engulfed me.

I was home.

THE RED LEATHER CHAIR

I left my office in the early afternoon and made my way down the High Street towards "Happy Joe's Sushi Bar." Across the road was the derelict town hall. I caught sight of a figure in the doorway that looked vaguely familiar. He was beckoning me. Curious, I crossed the road.

By the time I had negotiated the traffic, the figure had gone. I assumed he had entered the building. Inside, I walked through the dank, dirty hall. There was only the echo of my Italian brogues click-clacking on the bare oak floorboards, punctuated by the odd squeak as the wood protested against my presence.

In the dark recesses of the room, I was aware of scuttling creatures best left alone. I caught sight of what I hoped was furniture covered in greying dust sheets. The hall had a musty smell, like washing put away wet and then retrieved days or weeks later from a drawer. Unpleasant, but not overpowering.

The sun was struggling to light the room through filthy windows, but I could see a large mirror sitting above a fireplace at the far end of the hall. Tentatively poking out of a corner to the left of the fireplace was an uncovered armchair. Stepping closer, I saw that it was a red, leather armchair, crumpled with age and heavily stained. I turned to the mirror and wiped a significant amount of dust from the glass. I instantly regretted this as I hunted for a handkerchief to clean my hand. Movement caught my attention. In the mirror, some way behind me, was the figure I had seen outside the hall. The reason I was here.

"Hello there!" I said, turning to face my host. No reply. The figure shuffled towards me.

"Hello!" I repeated.

Still no reply. Slightly annoyed, I started towards the figure. As we neared each other, I noticed something wrong with this man's face. His eyes were sunken, and his mouth appeared to be in a fixed grimace. Odd. I peered closer and gasped in shock. The face was a macabre mixture of exposed skull and rotting blue-grey skin. His eye sockets were empty. Hollow blackness.

I backed away. My heart was beating too fast. I feared it might burst out of my chest. The butterflies in my stomach turned into birds, painfully flapping. This abomination shuffled forward, manipulating me into a corner. After an age of sliding backwards, unable to avert my eyes from the hideous face, I bumped, then fell into the red leather armchair. He was very close now. I could smell the aroma of death. There were rags hanging from a skeletal frame. I felt the cold hand of fear caress my neck. The figure loomed large. I could see nothing else. I was going to die...

The apparition shimmered like the air above a road on a hot day. As he shimmered, he vanished. The hall had changed; it was now occupied with people. Older people. It was obviously Christmas; there were gaudy decorations, a festive tree and a large table upon which sat the enormous cathedral-like carcass of a consumed turkey. A man stood up and silence descended. This man had an air of authority about him. He was wearing steel-rimmed spectacles and had a neatly clipped, white moustache which complimented his tidy, white hair. He was immaculately dressed in a crisp, light-blue shirt, and trousers with perfect creases. A military man, perhaps. From the red chair, I saw him turn and march to the crackling fireplace. He looked into the mirror, lost in his own thoughts and appeared unaware of his friends who were waiting expectantly. Without turning, he spoke.

"Bring him in then."

Two burly men dressed in Santa outfits walked over to a door situated on the same side of the room as my chair. They fumbled for a minute with a key. The door opened and they both reached in and pulled something out. It looked like an old potato sack with legs. I watched with mild amusement as they dragged the sack and contents to my chair. I jumped up suddenly when I realised that the bundle was being thrown into my seat. It then occurred to me that I was invisible to the crowd in the hall. I leant back against a wall to take in the show.

The sack was removed to reveal a sorry looking young man who was gagged and bound. My humour turned to deep concern as I studied the boy; he had been badly beaten. His eyes were bruised and swollen, and his nose was set at a strange angle, probably broken. His T-shirt was saturated with blood. He tried to rise but the two Santas held him down by his shoulders. On command from the man at the fireplace, they ripped off the silver tape from the boy's mouth. This re-opened cuts that criss-crossed his puffy lips. The boy let out a sorrowful whimper.

The man at the fireplace turned towards the youth. "I wish we all had fancy lawyers and rich fathers to get us out of trouble," he said morosely. "Everyone knows what you did to poor Gladys. You've been heard boasting about it to your rich friends. Some of them were eager to tell us what they knew." A stifled laugh echoed around the hall. The man continued. "You are no longer free. You are here to be judged. How do you plead to the murder of our friend, Gladys Digweed?"

The youth leant forward as far as he could. He cried out in pain, fear and defiance, "Get stuffed, you old bastards!"

"I had a feeling you might say that," said the man, allowing himself a sardonic smile. "Friends, what is the verdict?"

The word started quietly, whispered with glacial pace. As more joined in, the volume gathered speed. Louder and louder, to almost fever-pitch. Banging the table. Stamping their feet, the word reached a crescendo.

"GUILTY!"

The man moved towards the youth. In his hand was a poker. Attached to the end was a word crafted in fine metalwork. The word glowed white and amber with the heat. The Santas gripped the boy. The man neared, the poker outstretched. One Santa produced a knife and crudely cut off the youth's fringe to expose his forehead. The poker came ever closer. The boy screamed as the glowing wire kissed his skin with unbearable agony. I rushed forward to stop this torture. I grabbed at the man. I grabbed at nothing. He had gone.

I got up from the floor. I was alone in the hall. People, decorations, the youth. All gone. All gone... bar one. The apparition was still there. He stood staring at the redundant fireplace. He took no heed of me as I stood behind him. Looking in the mirror, I could see it. Time and surgery had removed it. I could see it as clearly as the day that the man had burnt it onto my skin. On my forehead, the word,

MURDERER.

It happened so long ago. I was the young man who had killed the old woman. I placed a hand on the man's shoulder, the man who had taken me back in time to remind me of what I had done, and whispered, "I'm so sorry."

I turned and left the room.

THE FACELESS ONES

"**G**ood morning, John. Have a seat."

"Thanks, Doc."

"Do you want me to stay, Doc?"

"No, thank you, Warden. Just secure John to the table, please. We'll be all right then."

"OK, Doc. I'll be outside. I'll knock in 45 minutes."

"How have you been, John, since our last meeting?"

"The tablets you've got me taking, I'm having lots of side effects."

"Such as?"

"I'm feeling on edge, Doc. I can't keep still. I can't relax. Sometimes I feel really high."

"OK, John. I will ask you to persevere with this medication. The side effects will weaken. I know it sounds odd, but I may increase the dosage to help you through the difficult adjustment period. Tell me about these trances you've been experiencing."

"What trances, Doc?"

"I have the warden's report here. On several occasions you've been observed in your cell, stood still, just staring at the wall. When attempts have been made to rouse you, you have started screaming. You have been shouting out 'Leave me alone. All of you.' Tell me what you're seeing."

"I don't really want to talk about it, Doc. Unless it goes no further."

"Of course not, John. There is still a doctor/patient confidentiality pact between us."

"My cell walls start to disappear. Brick by brick. As the walls vanish, the sun shines in.

"I close my eyes to the glare. The air smells sweet. It's like rose blossom and freshly cut grass, mixed together. I keep my eyes closed. I'm enjoying the warmth of the rays on my face. I hear birds, their beautiful chorus drifting on the soft breeze. I am free. I hear laughter. Innocent, joyful. I take in the scene. I am in a field. The yellow and white glimmer of a million buttercups and daisies light up the luscious green carpet. In the distance is a forest. All the trees seem to be one entity. Leaves of different hues mix in solidarity.

"A soft thumping of footsteps. A small figure is in front of me. Long pigtails bob up and down to the rhythm of a skipping rope. A red and white checked dress ends at the knee.

"I see young skin, unblemished by the weight of years or life.

"'Hello,' I call out. The figure keeps on skipping. She is singing. I listen carefully. I am surprised at her song.

"'Seasons don't fear the reaper, nor do the sun the moon or the rain. We can be like they are. Don't fear the reaper.'

"The contrast between her cherubic voice and the fatalistic tone of the song is startling. I move closer to her. She stops. She turns. She has no face. Where her features should be is a smooth canvass of skin. I step back. She steps forward. A sign begins to surface on her non-face. I watch as a question mark appears. She points to it. Her hand is just bone.

"'Are you the reaper, Mister?' she says, without a mouth.

"I pivot around. I want to run. Stopping me is a row of children. They are stood in my way.

"There are eight of them. Five children have normal faces with smiles to light up the heavens. The other three have the same blank visage as the skipping girl.

"As I watch, transfixed, the first child walks from behind me. She joins the others. As she does the children with faces step forward. Circles of rope are around their necks. These children start to jerk and spasm as the ropes tighten. Their eyes turn up into the lids, leaving just the whites visible. Their skin turns grey. Their lips turn blue. Finally, their tongues protrude with their last gasps. They fall to the ground. The fragrant meadow beneath their limp bodies opens up for moments. The children are swallowed by the earth. Then the holes seal themselves. All that remains is the gently rippling grass.

"The four that remain form a circle around me. They all have question marks on their blank faces. They hold hands. Their hands are all skeletal. They start to walk around me.

"'Where are we? Where are we?' they chant.

"They keep speaking the same words. I place my hands over my ears. It doesn't help.

"'Leave me alone!' I cry out. They stop and reach out for me. I fight them off. Only I'm not fighting them."

"OK, John. Relax. Follow my finger. Breathe deeply. Let me wipe the sweat off your brow."

"Sorry, Doc."

"That is all right, John. Have you thought about these visions? Have you tried to analyse the events?"

"There are nine of them in my vision. The same number of children that I strangled. I don't know why I would have started thinking of them."

"The five with faces, do you recognise them as some of your victims?"

"No."

"Why do you think that four of the children have no faces?"

"Couldn't tell you, Doc."

"We are running out of time, John. I'll cut to the chase. How many of the children that you killed were found?"

"They found five."

"Leaving four children unaccounted for. You have persistently refused to tell the authorities where the bodies are. Now the missing children are permeating your thoughts. Do you think..?"

"Very clever, Doc. You almost had me there. They found five. Good for them. I will take the locations of the other little bastards to the gas chamber. We're done. Guard!"

"You finished, Doc?"

"Yes, thank you, Warden. Please take John back to his cell."

"Come on, Strudwick. The boss is here to see you, Doc."

"Good morning, Governor."

"Hello, Frank. What progress with our child-killer?"

"The tablets I prescribed him produce a psychotic state. A mixture of sodium thiopental and klonopin. The former is better known as the truth drug. Klonopin will give John a high feeling. He will become restless. And more talkative."

"How long...?"

"Before he cracks, Governor?"

"We haven't got limitless time, Doctor."

"This is not an exact science. It is also unethical and illegal. I will persuade John to increase his dosage. I will see him daily. There is not much more I can do."

"I realise the risks you are taking, Frank. I am truly grateful. But before that son-of-a-bitch breathes his last I need to know where he buried those last children. I need to be able to look my wife and daughter in the eye. I need to be able to tell them that my granddaughter is coming home. For a burial where she belongs."

WATCHING FOR BADGERS

I always thought that I would be the strong one should disaster strike. When our son, Michael, was murdered, I fell to pieces. My wife, Claire, picked up those pieces. She cared for me and our twin girls, Olivia and Clara. She did everything. Shopping, cleaning, picking up the girls from pre-school. I remained in our bedroom. I was a disconsolate wreck. It was Claire and my brother, Peter, who approached me one day. They sat either side of me on the bed in Michael's old room. I had been spending a lot of time in there.

"Julian," said Claire, draping an arm around my shoulders, "I've arranged a move for us. A cottage out in the country. You don't have to do anything. Peter is going to help."

I looked at her. I was confused. Did I want to leave?

"You're not getting any better here. Let's get away," she said, pleading with me.

"Claire's right, old chap. We'll get you out of here," Peter murmured. "I'll be closer as well, to keep an eye on you."

I looked around Michael's empty room and then at Claire and Peter. "OK," I said.

Our cottage was one mile from the village of Littledean, situated in the Forest of Dean. It was a startling change to the city environment. I began to leave the house and take walks through the forest. Breathing in the country air cleared my mind.

I would stop at times. My patience was rewarded with sightings of roe and muntjac deer. I saw a wild boar one October day, foraging in the undergrowth. The sights and sounds of nature helped me forget. I began to pay more attention to Claire and the girls. I still grieved for Michael. I always would, but now I became a father and husband once more.

One night, Claire and I were alarmed at screams coming from the girls' room. We rushed in to find them under their quilts, crying.

"What's up, sweeties?" I said to the quivering lumps on the bed.

"There's something in the garden, Daddy."

Claire and I looked out. Something was out there. Two badgers roamed around the garden. Claire and I smiled at each other. She went downstairs and fetched a book on local wildlife. Once the habits and limitations of the creatures were explained, Olivia and Clara settled down.

The next night we were roused again. This time the girls were laughing and pointing at the badgers. Howls of disappointment erupted when they were tucked back into bed. I could see that getting them settled at night might become a problem. I decided to act.

I drove to the B&Q store in Gloucester. It felt surreal, being among people again. I concentrated on the task in hand. Purchasing the best CCTV system in the shop, I returned to the cottage and began work.

Before their bedtime, I showed Olivia and Clara what I had done that day. "During the night we can record the badgers and not miss their antics," I said, adding a little white lie. "If you don't go to sleep and the badgers see you, they will never come back. We wouldn't want that, would we?"

There was no noise from their room that night.

***

Olivia and Clara rushed in from pre-school the next day. "Daddy! Daddy! Did the badgers come?"

"Shall we see?" I replied.

We sat round all huddled together. I played the recording. It wasn't long before the badgers came into view. We sat there, each one of us fascinated by these creatures. A grainy image appeared on the screen. Just for a moment or two. It then vanished.

"Did you see that?" I asked Claire and the girls.

"See what, Julian?" replied Claire.

"There was some sort of figure on the screen. Did no-one else see it?"

Nobody had.

Later, I viewed the footage again on my own. There was definitely something alien on the recording. I could not make out the shape.

When watching the activities taking place in the back garden over the next few days, the shape on the recordings became clearer. Claire and the girls made no mention of it. I said nothing more about what I could see.

Watching a later film, I saw the figure again. This time it was very clear. The shape was illuminated by hundreds of small, white lights that formed the outside of the figure in three dimensions. It was a boy. He looked directly into the camera and spoke. I turned the sound to maximum. Sounding as if he was broadcasting on a radio with poor reception, the boy spoke again.

"Daddy! Where are you?"

It was Michael.

I hid the film and told Claire and the girls that the CCTV wasn't working properly. I said that I needed to stay in the garden that night to find out what was wrong and try to repair it.

That night, I sat on the back porch looking at the garden. The badgers came and, possibly alert to my presence, went. No sooner had they shuffled off out of sight then the lights began to appear. Slowly at first, a few at a time. Then their appearance gathered momentum until there was a blinding light, like the last cry of a dying sun.

After my temporary blindness had passed, there he was. Michael. We walked towards each other and stopped, neither of us sure how to proceed. Then Michael jumped up and I caught him. I could feel him but not his actual physical form. It was like hugging your favourite dream.

"Michael! I've missed you, so much," I sobbed.

I opened my eyes. He was no longer in my arms. Michael glided across the grass. His arms were outstretched, imploring.

"Daddy, don't let them hurt me."

The lights went out. I was alone.

What had he meant by 'them?' The man convicted of his murder had been in prison for several years now. Why did Michael not say 'him?' Thoughts like these pre-occupied my mind for the next few days. Claire told me that she and the girls were beginning to worry. They thought that I was breaking down again. For their sake I took another journey.

After applying for a visitor's pass online and being accepted, I drove to HMP Leyhill near Wotton-under-Edge, Gloucestershire. My visitor's pass was checked and I entered the visiting room. There he was, opposite me. The man who took the reason out of my life.

Anthony Hogg. Child murderer.

He spoke first. "I'm surprised to see you, Mr Des Barre."

He certainly looked much better than the pathetic creature who stood in the dock as the judge gave him a minimum sentence of 25 years.

"I don't want to be here any longer than necessary, Anthony, so I'll come to the point." I took a deep breath. "Did you murder my son?"

Hogg sat back in his chair, shocked at the question. "You were there at the trial. I pleaded guilty. I'm here now. What sort of question is that?" His raised voice caught the ear of a warder and he relaxed slightly.

"Anthony, I have information that you didn't kill Michael. Don't worry about where I got it from. I'm trying to help you. Please think back to that night. Anything else you can remember, now."

Hogg looked into my pleading eyes and relented. "I was on the park bench by the swings. I was sleeping rough in those days. I'd been staying on that bench for at least a week. I remember earlier that day as I had a good result, I'd nicked two bottles of white cider from the local corner shop. It was getting dark. I'd drunk both bottles. I was smashed. I dozed off. Then I heard a little boy, laughing. I looked but my eyes were really blurry. He climbed on a swing and someone behind him started to push."

"Someone else was there?" I interrupted. "You never mentioned that before."

"Julian," he said softly, "You have no idea what a mess I was at that time. I was drinking myself to death.

I had no idea what the last coherent thought I had was about. Can I finish?"

"I'm sorry. Please continue."

"I watched until I passed out. I woke up in a police cell. I was wearing one of those white, paper suits. The rest is history. I was covered in blood. I had a knife on me which I couldn't account for. I had very little idea about what I had been up to. I pleaded guilty for a reduced sentence. Here I am."

Hogg sat back in his chair. I wasn't satisfied. A man that drunk could not have possibly slit a boy's throat from behind and then stumble back to a bench and forget all about it. Who was the other person? Why did they leave my son alone in a park when it was getting dark? I leaned into Hogg. "I'm going to get you out of here. You did not do this."

Hogg grabbed my arm. "Listen here, Des Barre. I like it in here. Being in here saved my life. Do what you have to, but leave me out. Your boy's dead. I'm taking the rap. End of."

As I got up to leave, Hogg had one more nugget for me.

"Julian. As I've said, I don't remember much, but I'm pretty sure that the person with your son that night was a woman."

With my mind in turmoil, I contacted my brother, Peter. We were never that close, but he did have a way of rationalising problems. He kept his head when everyone was panicking. We met in a pub away from the village. I told Peter everything. When I had finished, he blew out his cheeks.

"That is one hell of a story," he said, eyebrows raised.

"You do believe me?" I replied.

"Of course I do, Julian. I just need to ask you. Are you sure you aren't having another breakdown?"

It was a fair question. "I'm positive. What am I going to do?"

Peter thought for a moment. "The first thing is to tell Claire."

***

When I returned from dropping the girls off at pre-school, Peter and Claire were sitting in the living room. A large glass of red wine had been poured for me. I took it and drained the glass. Claire took the empty glass into the kitchen and returned with it full. I took another generous swig and started to speak. Claire stopped me.

"Peter has told me everything. How could you?" she said, with steel in her voice. "You went behind my back. Why did you have to poke your nose into something that was finished?"

I finished my second glass. This time Peter refreshed it. I didn't know what to say. My mouth was dry. My eyesight started blurring. I took another drink, spilling most of it down my shirt. I tried to get up. I fell onto the floor. Raising myself unsteadily onto my hands and knees, I heard Claire speak.

"You are a fool, Julian. If only you had left well alone. Michael had to die. He found out about me and Peter. Worse still, he discovered that Olivia and Clara aren't your children. They're Peter's."

My head whirled with alcohol mixed with this devastating news. I tried to rise. My legs wouldn't obey me. I looked back up to Claire. Peter had now joined her, his arm around her waist. Claire had something in her hand. I shook my head vigorously to clear my vision. She had a noose in her hand.

They helped me through the house and back garden into the forest. I was too weak to resist them.

"Now, Julian, old chap," said Peter. "You can't get away. There was more than wine in your glass."

They took me to a tree some distance into the forest. They threw the noose around a branch. Then they hanged me. As I swung, I felt a small hand in mine. There was my son smiling up at me. He was hovering in the air.

"Let's go home, Daddy."

I am genuinely happy now. I spend all my time playing with Michael in the garden. We look like two Christmas trees running around. We both hope that Claire still watches the CCTV recordings. One day she may see more than badgers.

LEFT ON A PARK BENCH

Here I sit on my park bench
The only friend of mine
Sheltered by a mighty guardian
That caresses the sky
It leaves me insignificant in its wake

I have suffered slings and arrows
Bras dessus, bras dessous with misery
I've fallen into the abyss
Fingers grasping in the darkness
For the hope that never comes

People pass me by, not daring to stop
They sense the odour of my decay
Which is not made of cloth
It reaches far beneath
Deep, deep into the depths

With blank eyes I stare
Silken guano in my hair
The fruit of my guardian
Trying to awaken me
Not knowing of its failure

And still I sit no more to be
Memento mori to those who shun me
For two days past has my life gone
Into the ether of eternal sky
Mourned by none but my only friend.

*(This poem is based on an actual incident where a homeless
man died in a park in Southampton. To his memory.)*

LIFE'S A PICNIC

It is a day worthy of memory. The life affirming glow of the sun. Frisbees and balls flying through the air. The sweet smell of summer grass. Rugs laid over the ground. Expectant mouths. The scene permeates my body. I take a second to sigh contentedly. Looking around for my children, I spot them by some litter bins. They are being chased by much bigger kids. They are trying to hit my children with cricket bats and tennis racquets. I shouldn't even think about my next move. I am scared. The big kids are also a lot larger than me. Perhaps they'll leave my family alone.

The attack continues. I fight my fear and rush over. I chase the antagonists. For a moment I appear to have won. Two of the brutes flee. Feeling very smug, I turn to my kids.

"Look out, Dad!" they cry in unison. Too late. I receive the full force of a flailing bat. Falling to the ground I see a blurred shape coming in for the kill. Is this death?

"Peter, get away from those bins. Come and have something to eat." These maternal words save me. Peter responds to his mother's tongue. He leaves. My children rouse me. We search for a spot away from our attackers.

"Are all picnic rugs tartan in design?" I ask myself before I start on a bread roll. Jam. My favourite. The children hover very close by. They fight over a piece of fruit. I keep a wary eye on them. I hardly notice the darkness descending. It spreads quickly, consuming all. The children haven't noticed it. I try to call to them. They don't hear me. The foot stamps hard on the ground. It squashes the piece of fruit.

The light is back. I wish it wasn't. Among the remnants of juice and pips is my family. They have been pulverised beyond recognition. My children are a mangled mess of bodily fluids, perforated with the odd body part. I must take revenge.

Flying stealthily, I find the foot's owner. He is too engrossed in filling his fat face. I swoop in. My sting makes its mark. I soar away as a hand slaps at my mark.

"What's the matter, John?"

"I've just been stung by a bloody wasp."

Yes! Take that, murderer. Now, I am sure I saw another jam sandwich nearby.

PICK A PICKLED PEPPER

(Inspired by Barbara's garden.)

Ay up. Time to close the shop for good. T'is bloody chilly tonight. I haven't seen a soul all evening. One final look at the sign that's been hanging there for nigh on 40 years.

RUTH AND ALBERT HODGES
FRIENDLY FAMILY GREENGROCERS

We managed to survive even when they opened a Tesco shop up the road. I started not to care when my Ruthy died. It's time I went. Suitcases are packed; passport and money in hand luggage; bank account transferred. Shop sold. One thing left. Should I deal with the little problem in the basement? Or shall I be on me way?

I wouldn't have put them there. They only had to leave Ruthy alone. Towards the end Ruthy wasn't right. In the head. She'd forget things. I would find unopened tins in the oven, ready to explode. She would go out without shoes. She was always strong, my Ruthy. She told me not to fuss. That she was all right. I was scared. I knew she was ill.

One day, she came back from the post office. She was wide-eyed, pale and trembling.

"What's the matter, Ruth?" I said, taking her hand gently.

"They took my pension, Albie."

"Who took your pension?"

"Three of them. One young lady and two fellas. They said we owed them money from the shop. I gave them everything, Albie. I'm so very sorry."

As she wept, I held her close to me. "It's all right, my Ruthy. It's all right," is all I could say.

I was having a break in the kitchen not long after this robbery when Ruthy screamed out for me from the shop. As I jumped, the tea in my hand splashed on my shirt. I rushed to her. She was behind the counter, shaking like a small child during a violent thunderstorm. She had wet herself.

Near to the door stood two men and a woman. The woman spoke first. "We all had a little visit from the old bill. Somethin' about her pension money." She pointed menacingly at Ruth. I moved in front of my wife.

"Just a friendly warning," she continued. "If we're bothered again by the filth, we'll be back. Next time we'll take more than your stinkin' pension."

She stared at us for a few moments. On their way out, one of the men kicked over a display bin of apples. I closed the shop.

Sunday afternoon was our time together. We'd walk in the park, then have lunch. Occasionally, we would go to the movies. That Sunday, we went to the shopping arcade. I remember Ruth needed a new hat for a christening. Coming out of a shop, I heard her gasp and she gripped my arm tightly. Walking towards us were our three antagonists.

"No. No," cried Ruth.

"It's OK, Ruth. They won't hurt us here. Let's just walk away."

Ruth was terrified. My words couldn't calm her. She broke free of my grip and ran. She didn't run very far. The car didn't have a chance of stopping. All my dear wife once was, was now a bloody wad laying on a dirty road.

The 40-watt bulb hardly lights the cellar. I spent hours in here. Moving stock up and down those rickety stairs. It's a wonder I didn't break me bleedin' neck. Nothing in here now. Except my three guests. I had to pick them off one by one. A lot of work. Looking at them now it was worth it. They are bound to the table where Ruthy used to trim the caulies. Their heads and hands poke through the stocks I built. Everything secured. It must be damned uncomfortable. I've also made little alleyways topped with chicken wire. These run from one side of the table right up to their faces. I got the idea from my favourite book, 1984. They don't know what's coming.

This final memory of Ruthy moistened my eyes. It spurred me on for the final conclusion. As I ripped the duct tape from their mouths, I was met with a torrent of abuse. Some of it directed at Ruth. It made what I was about to do easier. From under the table, I retrieved three huge peppers. Red, green and yellow. I placed one each at the end of the three alleyways that lead to their faces. They fall silent.

"Inside one of these peppers is a very nasty surprise," I said, taking turns to look at each of them. "I will let the lady choose first. Pick a colour."

The 'lady' declined.

"Let me make myself clear. You will stay here cold, hungry and sat in your own filth until you pick. I have plenty of time."

I heard a weak sound.

"Come again?" I said.

"Yellow!" shouted the woman.

I placed the yellow pepper at her tunnel. I pulled the tape from the top and took it off. The look of terror on her face as a Fattail scorpion crawled slowly out gave me a warm feeling. The glass-shattering scream increased my delight. The scorpion has poor eyesight. It also has excellent hearing. It homed in on the whimpering at the end of the alley. It stung. Repeatedly. The woman fell unconscious. This type of scorpion is fatal. Her two companions started pleading for their freedom. I placed the remaining two peppers in front of them. I let the contents out. A black widow spider and a northern death adder. I turned the light off and left them to get acquainted.

The driver put my bags into the boot of his taxi. I gave the shop one goodbye glance. On the way to the airport, I smiled.

I waited until I was in the boarding lounge. I texted numbers that I had retrieved from the mobile phones of the three thugs. I provided enough information for someone to find my Ruthy's killers. Before I boarded the plane for Rio de Janeiro, I threw the phone away. A new life beckoned. A sad, empty life.

JENNIFER THX

My sight is blurry. I open my eyes. There is a cacophony of bleeps, buzzes, whirrs and whistles. As the mist vanishes, I realise that I'm in a factory. Machinery of all shapes and sizes in constant motion. It feels more like an operating theatre. A sterile atmosphere. I try to look around but cannot move my head. From my peripheral vision, I can discern that I am on a conveyor belt, moving slowly. I try to call out. There is no sound from my open mouth. I try to remember how I came to be here. My mind throws up a brick wall. I try to move. I cannot feel my limbs. I am paralysed.

Terror grips me. In a factory. Unable to move. What is going to happen to me? The conveyor belt glides to a stop. My eyes dart around in their sockets, looking for clues. I feel a needle enter the back of my head. Then a dull sensation. Oh God! Someone is opening up my head. I cannot scream but I can cry. Big drops cascade down as I feel fingers inside my skull. It lasts forever. Over quickly. An object has been placed inside my brain. My head is closed. The conveyor belt resumes its journey.

As I travel, my mind clears. Tiptoeing through remnants of buildings and bodies, two children hold my hands. My children. We scream as another laser bolt rips through the city. It out-shouts the siren that warns of the carnage to come. I leave them at a concrete bunker, a school. I make promises to return and although their pained looks break my heart, I must pick up our allotted provisions. They get smaller every week that this conflict continues. A soldier approaches and he stops me. We converse. I notice his colleague far too late to act. A cosh falls heavily. Then blackness.

New thoughts invade. I see scenes of battle and bloodshed. Images of weaponry. Of its component parts. Maps and charts of the earth and the solar system. They imprint themselves without invitation. The pain of this forced information stops in sync with the conveyor belt. My head is gripped either side. I am lifted up. My reflection stares from the polished surface of a machine. My long hair has gone. Wires and tubes are attached to my shaven head. I look further. I have no body. I am just a head suspended in the air. Still no scream.

My head is carried towards a suit of armour. Gently, I am lowered onto this metal body. The grips retract from my skull. They are replaced by a large hoop which lowers around my neck. Various tools extend from this circle. They start to work. I feel the sensation. No pain. The tools finish abruptly. The loop disappears. I now have a body. I am whole. Only restricted movement. I turn my head left and right. Other heads are being placed on artificial carcasses. This soothes me. I am not alone. I am propelled forward. As I travel, I acquire a helmet. A visor descends over my eyes. I can see more clearly. Not far away is a row of boxes. Human-sized sarcophagi. The doors slowly open. I read the words written on them.

JENNIFER THX SERIES ONE
COMBAT READY CYBORG.

I am placed inside. The door shuts. My new life begins.

THE POWER OF THREE,
CHRIS' STORY

I was ten years old when I discovered my power. Playing in my bedroom, I knocked a chest of drawers and a large glass container of marbles hurtled towards the floor. I closed my eyes and visualised the container floating in the air. I imagined it gliding down to the ground intact. When I opened my eyes, the container, with its contents, was resting by my feet. Confused and frightened at what had happened, I cried out in fear. My mother rushed into the bedroom.

"Christopher, what's the matter?" she said, concerned.

I looked at the marbles. I looked at my mum.

"Nothing, Mum. I'm sorry."

I searched for answers on my computer. I typed in 'moving objects with the mind'. The answer came.

Telekinesis. User can influence/manipulate/move matter with their mind. Telekinesis is one of the basics of many superpowers that are based on controlling/manipulating, and may evolve to the point that a telekinetic can control anything at a sub-atomic level.

Basic levels include the ability to: Keep objects from being moved, levitate objects, project objects as bullets, strangle others.

Advance levels include: Manipulate the movement of others, unlock doors and other internal mechanisms, make an object explode, to use telekinesis to fly, to manipulate matter not within the user's location, i.e. through the medium of television.

I digested all the information. Scrolling down, I discovered films had been made on this subject. I had to see them. My father had an extensive collection of films. Among them a listed film, *Carrie*.

As soon as I was able, I watched *Carrie* alone in my room. It concerned a girl who had the power of telekinesis. She was also a loner, ostracized by her school friends. Her ability to move objects and people by the power of her mind grew throughout the film. The film culminated in a mass slaughter at a school prom brought about by her telekinetic power. I was terrified. I did not want to be like this girl. I vowed never to publicly display my capability.

***

Walking to the shops at the end of the school day. I go to the store this time of day as the sound of children laughing, singing, whooping with delight fills me with joy. They hug their parents. Some chatter about the events of the day. Some cry about a small slight they have suffered or a minor graze on a dirty knee. Realising I'm staring, I continue my journey. Who knows why the boy ran into the road. The traffic is slow and condensed but the 4x4 heads towards him...

I could have saved the child. I have practised my power away from prying eyes in forests or back allies in the depths of night. I let him die for my own selfish needs. I live as a hermit now. I work from home; I shop at dusk. This power has imprisoned me.

***

Life changed when I met Liz. We weren't paying attention and bumped our shopping trollies together.

"I'm sorry," I said, "I wasn't looking where I was going."

"Don't worry," she replied, "I'm always in a daydream."

There was an awkward silence.

"Do you come here often?" I finally said.

A broad smile spread across her face.

"Oh god!" I exclaimed, "I didn't mean to use such an old cliché. I mean, it wasn't a chat up line or anything like that."

Liz started to laugh at my discomfort. "It's OK," she said, lightly touching my arm. "Walk with me."

That was how our relationship started. We met regularly at the supermarket. We were two lonely people, one by his own choice, the other through bad luck. After meeting in these circumstances several times, Liz asked me out. I agreed. I had been lonely for too long.

We eventually moved into a flat. I was so happy. I had never done anything wrong, but I thought of my ability as a curse. Now I barely thought about it. Liz was always happy. She was fun. Her joie de vivre was infectious. I was alive.

I met Liz outside the school where she taught. As we walked hand in hand, the young children swarmed past us, playing and shouting. Their carefree nature made me smile. Liz caught my smiling face. "Do you think that one day we might...?"

I interrupted her. "Yes. I love you. I can think of nothing better."

We turned to embrace. A scream. A mother's scream. I looked up. A child fallen in the road. Please, not now. My eyes closed. The child was in my mind. I made him hover above the ground. I quickly moved him to the pavement. I opened my eyes. Due to me, the car had missed him.

"Come on, let's go," I said to Liz, pulling her sharply along.

We walked home in silence. I was hoping that the incident by the school would not be discussed up. Liz had other ideas.

"I saw that little boy float above the ground and then whizz to the kerb. Did you not see it?"

"Liz, I was paying more attention to you. Do you really want children with me?"

"Don't change the subject, Chris. I'm sure you were looking."

"I wasn't. Leave it alone!"

I instantly regretted shouting at Liz. She forgave me. It would be the first and last time I ever raised my voice to her.

***

Liz arranged our holiday that year. We stayed at a bed and breakfast in Lulworth, Dorset. We made love on the beach under a waning sun. We rushed into the sea splashing each other with childlike glee. I was free from my guilt; the burden had faded. Walking together along the Dorset coastline, we approached the Durdle Door rock. The sun had lit up a million diamonds resting on the calm surface of the sea. Other holiday makers were admiring the view or having picnics. The day was made perfect when Liz stopped me.

"I'm pregnant, Chris."

I yelled out in joy. This was what I wanted. A family. I hugged her. I spun her around like a top. "Thank you, Liz. Thank you," I said breathlessly as I set her down.

"I'm glad you're happy. I need to ask you something important. Would you always keep us safe?"

"Yes, of course I would. What do you mean, Liz?"

"I saw how you saved that boy outside of the school. I'm not stupid, Chris. Would you do the same for me and your child?"

I couldn't think of anything to say. I stared blankly at Liz. She had discovered the secret I had tried to hide. After an interminable silence she spoke. "Let's see what you will do."

Liz turned towards the cliff face and ran. She jumped over the edge. The rocks below waited for her. There were screams and shouts. I closed my eyes and focused. Hard.

Liz stood next to me. I could hear voices nearby, uttering comments. "Did you see that?", "I don't believe it.", "I've caught it on my phone."

I looked at Liz. "I knew you would save us, Chris. I just knew it."

I took Liz by the shoulders. "What have you done?" I said. "I have kept this secret for most of my life. Now everyone is going to know. My life will never be the same again. You've ruined me."

I left Liz and walked across the rocky outcrop of Durdle Door. I stared down at the sea.

I thought I heard Liz calling my name. I stepped off to embrace the rocks.

They never found my body. Of course they didn't. It never hit the rocks. I've started a new life, far away.

I miss Liz but I can't forgive her. Throwing herself off the cliff that was a despicable trick to play. I think I will remain alone now. Just me and my power.

THE POWER OF THREE, ELIZABETH'S STORY

I knew that Chris survived his leap from the cliff face. I can foresee when people are close to death. I've had this ability since I was a young girl. Chris wasn't near to his end. I don't think Chris knew about my power.

I didn't know about it myself, until the time I went to stay with my nan.

I loved my nan. She gave me all the comfort and love that I never received from my mum and step-dad. I would sit on her knee while she told me stories.

The same scene always played out. The doorbell rang. It was be my mum. Drunk. Again.

"I see you are in your normal state," Nan said.

"Piss off, you old bat," my mum replied.

"It's not right that you pick up Liz when you are so drunk. You can't even look after yourself."

"Just give me my bloody kid. I don't need lectures from you."

Then Nan's voice mellowed. "Why don't you let me look after Liz. I'll bring her back later, when you've rested."

My mum barged past Nan and grabbed me. As I left with Mum, Nan would always say the same thing. "I love you, my little Lizzie. Come back soon."

Home life was not good. My real dad had died, and Mum married this terrible man, Frank. He seemed to be perpetually pissed. I am sure that he encouraged Mum to join him in this eternal bliss. He hit me, when he could catch me. Mum would cover up the bruises and beg me not to say anything at school, but the teachers weren't stupid. They realised what was happening. I was confronted by the police and social services. Under their questions I broke down and the truth came out in a torrent of hidden pain. Mum and Frank were arrested. I never saw them again. There was some great news for me. I was allowed to live with Nan.

It was a bitter winter's day when I came home from college and found Nan in bed. She stirred as I crept up to her. "There you are, Lizzie. I'll get up and make some tea."

"It's all right, Nan. Let me do that. You stay in bed."

As I closed the door, I looked back at her. It hurt me to see her looking so sallow and frail. Without warning the room changed. It was dark. The curtains were pulled. Nan was lying on the bed. She was lifeless. As I rushed towards her, the room reverted. Nan roused temporarily and went back to sleep.

The image was distressing. It stayed with me all day at college. I put it down to my vivid imagination. This was difficult. The picture of Nan lying dead was so clear.

***

After college, a group of us went to a local bar but I wasn't in the mood for socialising. I made my excuses and left.

When I arrived home, it was dark. There were no lights on in the house. A pang of guilt washed over me. I should have come home earlier. "Nan! It's me, Lizzie. You all right?"

I tiptoed up the stairs. I opened the door quietly. The room was dark. The curtains were closed. Nan was in bed. Dead.

Nan left me everything in her will. I was now very comfortably well-off. This didn't help me much. I missed her. She occupied my thoughts constantly. At night, I remembered the image of her passing. It was only a day before her actual death. Did I foresee her death? I had to find out. To do this I did something quite callous.

During the few weeks that I worked voluntarily in a home for older people my fears were confirmed. I saw the imminent deaths of many of the residents. I had visions of people dying in bed or sitting in their chairs. One gentleman died falling down the stairs. I felt some remorse for this man. Could I have saved him? Who would believe me if the truth came out? Exhausted, I left the home. I was tired of all the death.

My work, teaching at a primary school, kept me busy. I believed that my illusions of death were restricted to those who were probably near to their demise. By working with young people, I could forget about the past. I was kidding myself. Children die whether by accident or natural causes. I was hoping that death wouldn't visit any of my children.

Running late one morning, I arrived at the bus stop just in time. As I waited on the bus to buy my ticket, I looked for a space among the crowded seats. I didn't see a vacant seat. What I did see was the mangled, bloodied bodies of the passengers. The image was fleeting but real. I turned, pushed past the people behind me and ran all the way home.

Watching the evening news confirmed my worst nightmare. The bus had been in a terrible pile-up. There were no survivors. I screamed and cried. I tried to make sense of it all. The bulletin mentioned that there were children among the dead. I was wrong.

I moved away from the area. The flat I bought was small. It became my sanctuary and my prison. Days were spent watching the television. Nights were pretty much the same, except for a weekly sojourn to a late-night supermarket. It was there that I met Chris.

Walking around the store, I half-expected an interrogation under the artificial glare of the lights. The gentle humming of the freezers was strangely comforting. Apart from the drone of daytime television, I didn't usually hear much else. It had become my habit to shop while avoiding any eye contact. It was no surprise when I bumped my trolley into someone else's.

"I'm sorry," I said, breaking my custom and looking up at my fellow shopper.

"I'm sorry," replied the man in front of me. "I wasn't looking where I was going."

The man had a strong jawline and a nose that was slightly out of shape. From his facial features and physique, I imagined that he was a rugby player. He was tall, broad-shouldered and lean. I looked into his eyes. There was a sadness to them.

"Do you come here often?" he said.

I smiled.

"Oh god!" he exclaimed. "I'm not trying to chat you up or anything."

I started to laugh at his discomfort. "That's all right," I said. "Walk with me."

Chris was incredibly shy. After a few encounters in the shop, I ended up asking him out. He would quite often avoid eye-contact. Sometimes when the conversation would dry up, Chris would start rubbing the back of his head. He had been alone for too long. So had I.

Over the coming weeks, Chris and I became more comfortable with each other. We moved in together later that year. I was so content. I returned to teaching at a local primary school. Chris would often meet me after work. It was on such an occasion that I discovered something very special about him.

The children ran past us, laughing and playing as we walked home, arm in arm. I turned to Chris. "Do you think that maybe..?"

He interrupted me. "Yes. I can think of nothing better."

My daydreams of motherhood ended abruptly with a scream. A boy had fallen in the road. I heard the desperate screech of car brakes. I saw the boy levitate. I saw him fly towards the pavement and land safely. I turned to Chris. His eyes were closed and his face had a look of total concentration. He slowly opened his eyes and looked at the boy. He grabbed my elbow roughly. "Come on, Liz. Let's go home."

After a walk home in silence, I tried to raise the subject of the boy. Chris didn't want to discuss it and shouted at me. He quickly apologised. I knew that I had touched a raw nerve. Chris was hiding something.

The next day, I saw the boy who had fallen in the road. I asked him what had happened. He told me that he wasn't quite sure. He felt as if someone had picked him up, threw him to the pavement and then gently set him down. As the boy walked away from me, I realised that I had not foreseen his death.

Despite us trying for a baby, our relationship had become tense. I felt that I had uncovered a secret that Chris had been desperate to keep. My suspicion that Chris had saved the boy was confirmed late one evening. I had gone to bed leaving Chris watching television. I got up later for a drink of water. Chris was still on the settee. I watched him for a while. I was still crazy about him. As he stood up, he knocked the coffee table. A bottle of wine toppled over. Before it reached the floor, it stopped in mid-air and then travelled gracefully back to the table. I quickly and quietly returned to the bedroom.

We went to Lulworth that summer. The holiday atmosphere had melted any remaining friction between us. Our days were spent mainly walking along the glorious coastline. It was on one such occasion that I decided to test my theory.

We were strolling towards the Durdle Door rock when I stopped him. "Chris, I'm pregnant."

His reaction startled me. He whooped with joy. He picked me up and spun me around. He even thanked me. I then put my plan into action. After forcing him to say that he would always keep me and the baby safe, I jumped from the cliff edge.

I didn't fall far. I felt as if a giant pair of hands had cradled me. They took me up towards the cliff edge and deposited me next to Chris. He wasn't happy to see me. There had been witnesses. I hadn't counted on that. Someone had even filmed the incident on their mobile phone. Chris accused me of ruining his life. He slowly walked across the Durdle Door. He stepped off.

I never saw Chris again. I tried to call him a couple of times, but he made it quite clear that he no longer wanted me in his life. I begged him for the sake of our child. He said that he doubted that I was even pregnant. He was on his own and that was how he wanted his life to be. Heartbroken, I moved away. There is one thing left for me now. He fills the Chris-shaped void in my life. Our son. Wayne.

***

There was always a fear that Wayne would inherit the gifts possessed by his parents. There was nothing to show this in his formulative years. He caught childhood illnesses. He cried, slept and laughed. He went to pre-school. He made friends and I made friends. Chris began to fade into a foggy memory. Then Wayne went to junior school...

I can't place exactly when he changed but change he did. As he rushed towards puberty, he became more reclusive, aggressive. I guessed it was the difficult period of growing up and tried to explain. Wayne did not want to know. He became abusive towards me.

On a rare outing together, we were sat outside a café in a local park. I had a latte and a cigarette, Wayne a coke. I closed my eyes and faced towards the sky. The sun christened me with its rays. The smell of cut grass was sweet and for a while I was a child again, experiencing these sensations for the first time. Raised voices trespassed into this world. Wayne was in a heated row with a boy that he did not get on with. I knew the boy and his mother who was present and pushing her young daughter in a push chair.

"You're a fucking loser," shouted Wayne at the boy. "Your mum's had more pricks than a second-hand dart board."

"Wayne, you apologise at once," I screamed, grabbing hold of his collar. He turned to face me. I was afraid. His eyes were red and trying to bulge from his head. A deep blue vein pulsed in his temple like a drumbeat. Spittle had formed on his lips like scum on the shore of a dirty sea. He pulled away. "Get the fuck off me!" he shouted and pulled free into the path of the other boy. The boy grabbed Wayne's throat and drew back his fist. It never found its target. The boy floated into the air. Five, ten feet, maybe more. His terror increased as he plummeted to the ground. I almost vomited as I saw blood spread from his prone body. It was an eternity until he staggered to his feet, shook his head and shuffled away. His mother went to follow him, but Wayne stopped her push chair. I saw her take a frightened gasp of air. Wayne looked into the chair at the now crying infant. He looked at the woman with a face cold with spite. "She's going to die soon, that little brat of yours."

***

The little girl did die. It was on the news, a tragic swimming pool accident. We were not in the area at the time. As soon as we had returned home from the park, I packed up our lives and we went far away. I schooled Wayne at home. My shopping was delivered. I never socialised again. Wayne must never leave the house.

THE POWER OF THREE, WAYNE'S STORY

I shuffled through my old prison. I was the gaoler. My only inmates were memories. I recalled looking through the window at the sun. I longed to feel its loving embrace on my skin. I listened to the rain fall. I ached to dance, to laugh, as it cleansed me. Was I the gaoler or still a prisoner?

I didn't organise a wake. She didn't have any friends anyway. Not even me. I hated her for what she had done. My first trip outside is to bury the person who had incarcerated me. The irony forces a bitter smile. She left me everything. This gloomy flat. Her meagre possessions. And her 'gift'.

***

I grew too strong for her. I was leaving. She grabbed my arm and begged like a leper. I shook her off. My hand was on the first chain to the front door.

"You have a power, Wayne," she blurted out.

I turned around. "What are you talking about, you old hag?"

"Your father and I both had special abilities. I know that you have at least one of them. Your father could will objects, even people, to move."

She was right. I did have the power to move objects simply by thinking of them. I had knocked over a drink in the lounge once. I imagined it hovering in the air and then back on the table. That was what happened. I had been honing this skill in the loveless loneliness of my room ever since.

"And the other?"

She paused and looked nervously at the floor. When she looked up, she had an air of timid defiance. "My power is why I kept you safe. Why I schooled you at home. Why-"

"What is it, bitch! Why have you ruined my life?"

I didn't care about the tears sprouting from this pathetic woman. I needed the answer.

"I can see when people are about to die," she said feebly. "I have seen some terrible sights. I wanted to protect you."

The next couple of hours were spent with her explanations. She foresaw the death of her nan. The bus accident. My father plunging over a cliff. When she had finished, I stared deeply into her eyes.

"What a load of bollocks," I replied.

"Wayne, you must believe me."

"I don't believe a word you've said. You kept me in this shit-hole because I can move a few ornaments around without touching them. So what?" If the figure next to me hadn't looked so pathetic I might have struck her.

"I'm going to bed. Tomorrow I am out of here," I said.

I disappeared into my room.

I passed through the lounge during the night. I glanced briefly at her asleep on the sofa. Returning with my glass of water, I stopped to examine her. She was snoring. She was lying face down on the sofa. Empty pill bottles littered the floor. A bottle of scotch was on the table. Empty. I stepped back. She was snoring again.

I found her the next morning. Pill bottles and an empty bottle of scotch. I felt a strange sensation. Relief mixed with a pinch of sadness. I was free. With two extraordinary gifts.

The telekinesis was proven but the other gift? I started to wait outside old people's homes watching as the oldies went on with their pointless lives. I saw the deaths of those who still existed. Brilliant! What to do next.

I spent a while considering how to make my abilities profitable. Not much money to be made seeing dead people. What could I move to make money? I needed to keep this power under wraps. I did not want to become a media freak-show. I certainly did not wish to become a military experiment. What to do?

Idly watching sport on a Saturday afternoon, I found the answer. People spend a great deal of money betting on the outcome of sport. I could change the course of a sporting event and bet on it accordingly. I had research to complete. And practise.

I focused on boxing matches. I could force one opponent's arms down. This would render him help-less against any onslaught. I could do this from home, in front of the television. I made reasonable amounts at first. What I was waiting for was a big fight. A fight with a clear underdog. A fight with overwhelming odds.

Nothing stirs the boxing fraternity like a world title fight. Add in the glamour of Las Vegas, and the rich and famous froth at the mouth. Make the contest a heavyweight bout and the world sits up and takes notice. A young, unbeaten American against an older

Mexican. Some bookmakers had stopped taking bets on the American. This was a sure thing.

I made a large wager at the bookmakers on the day of the fight. All my money was on the Mexican winning by a knock-out. I went home and made myself comfortable. I was nervous as I turned on the telly. My plan could fail, and I would lose a lot of money.

The Mexican came into the arena. His face had suffered a lot of punishment. He was flabby. He was perfect. The American was an impressive sight. He was chiselled from granite with a body of perfect tone and symmetry. They were face to face in the ring. The Mexican was six feet and two inches tall and 17 stone. The American towered over him. Then a vision of what was to come. The ring was full of concerned faces. The American was motionless on the canvas. Blood seeped from his ears. His lifeless eyes saw nothing. Then back to the present as the American sneered at the Mexican as they touched gloves. The bell rang.

By the end of the third round, the Mexican was a sight to behold. His ringside team were desperately stemming his blood. It flowed from cuts expertly ripped open around his eyes. A large mound had sprung up on his left cheek. It was a sign of the power and accuracy of an American fist. A doctor was called. He examined the Mexican closely. I was no longer nervous. I knew the outcome.

Before the bell for the fourth round, I made a call. My bet was now on the Mexican knocking out his tormenter during the next three minutes. The bookmaker must have been sporting a huge grin as he took my instructions.

I allowed the American a few jabs into the Mexican's face. The latter lumbered forward. He swung a wild punch. The blow connected. The American staggered. With his opponent unable to defend himself, the Mexican surged forward. I do occasionally wonder what the American was thinking. There he was, unable to raise his arms. Punch after punch smashing his features. His face became an unrecognisable pulp. The final blow found the American's right temple. Mouthguard, spit and blood flew across the ring. I turned the television off before the American hit the floor.

I did have some trouble collecting my winnings. Questions were asked due to the unusual circumstances surrounding the fight. There was even an article in the local paper. I passed it all off as a lucky hunch. Then I laughed on my way to the bank.

On my way back from another indulgent shopping spree a few days later, there was a stranger on my doorstep.

"Can I help you, mate?" I said, thinking that he was another reporter.

"Hello, Wayne. No easy way to say this. I'm your father."

The guy looked ashen and drawn. He was wearing clothes that were years out of date. If it hadn't been daylight, I would have thought that he was a vampire. He looked weak like a streak of piss. No problem here. "You're Darth Vader, are you? Better come in, but you ain't staying for long."

He sat down on the sofa. I did not offer him any refreshments.

"You're my daddy, are you?" I said derisively. "I thought you were dead."

He stood up and walked thoughtfully around the room. He stared out of the window. With his back to me, he finally spoke. "I know more about you than you realise. I am here to save you from yourself."

I was already weary of this conversation. "Will you get to the point or get out?" I snapped.

When he turned around, he was holding a pistol. Pointed at me. "The fateful boxing match, that was you."

I said nothing. I wasn't surprised. How many others had powers like ours? I was getting bored with this visit.

"I watched the replay," he continued. "I read the newspaper article. A boxer suddenly unable to move his arms. A huge wager placed by you to coincide with the final outcome. What sickens me is that you knew that young fighter was going to die, but carried on anyway. You are a murderer."

"Like father like son," I replied. "If you are going to shoot me, get on with it."

"I'm not going to kill you, son. I will make sure that you can't harm anyone else."

He flicked his mobile open. Still aiming his gun at me he made a call. "Hello, police? A man has been shot at flat two, 23, Royal Mews. He may be dead. Please get here quickly."

He put his mobile away. He stood there in silence. I broke that silence.

"Go on. Shoot me, you bastard. Don't just stand there. Do it!"

He did nothing. I wasn't scared until I heard the sirens. He had to act soon. I closed my eyes.

"Here, catch," he said. He threw the gun to me.

I instinctively caught it. I pointed at him. "The boot's on the other foot now, old man. I'm not going to kill you. I'll let the old bill deal with you. Breaking in and threatening me with a gun. You'll do time."

Heavy knocking at the door. "Police! Open up!"

I tried to turn. I was paralysed. I tried to resist as my right arm raised the gun.

"There is only one bullet in that gun. It was never meant for you. Enjoy prison life."

The front door flung open. The police entered. My father's last act was to force my trigger finger. He fell lifeless to the floor. I felt many hands on me.

***

I've come full circle now. I started this story in a gaol kept away from the outside world and now I'm back in one. This time it's at Her Majesty's pleasure and my room is not like my old room. This one's a steel one with nice padding. I wish I was back home.

HUNT THE PIPER

I sit in front of the panel. It's another review. I do not know why they bother. It always ends the same. They ask the perfunctory questions. I give the perfunctory replies. Three of them deliberate. I prepare for a return to my cell. My home. The head of the panel, Dr Schweiz, looks up. A calm man. A studied man. Cool and composed. A bastard.

"Well, Jean," he stresses, taking off his spectacles for effect. "From all the reports we have collected and the general consensus of the staff, I think you can go home."

The decision hits me hard in the stomach, like a freight train. "Home?" I reply.

"Yes, home," he replied with a new softness in his voice. "You will still be under the care of this clinic for some time. Nurse Carter will arrange appointments with you. Good luck, Jean."

He stands and reaches out his hand. I'm sobbing. I shake his hand. I turn and leave.

I feel like an intruder entering my house. Jeff, my husband, is not there. The last thing he did was to make sure I had a home. I'll visit him with some flowers later. I open the bedroom door. A multitude of ghosts are present.

Jeff is laying on the bed. He is wearing nothing but a school cap. "You have some homework to do, teacher," he says.

Christmas day. I open a stunning, diamond necklace from Jeff. He opens his present. It is a bib and a packet of nappies.

He looks puzzled. The mist clears. "You're pregnant! I'm so happy," he said, wiping the tears away from his face.

A Siberian winter's day. Jeff rushes into the bedroom. I'm lying distraught on the bed. He lays to next to me. "I'm so sorry, Jeff," I whisper.

"It's all right, Jean. We'll try again. When you are ready. If you want to."

I erupt with fresh tears. "The doctors have told me that was the only chance we had. Please forgive me."

Jeff took me in his arms. He looked into my tearstained face. "There is absolutely nothing to forgive. We still have each other. Forever."

I look in the dressing table mirror. Even with grey hair and harsh facial lines, I am presentable. Perhaps there is still a life for me. I learned to control my fear of The Piper in the clinic. I turned it into hate. A cold, simmering fury. Even so, The Piper still invades my dreams. He has been a part of my life for so long, I don't know anything else.

I am awake again at two in the morning. The cigarette tastes like ash in my mouth. I have made a decision.

I take a flight to Dusseldorf. A three-hour train journey follows. It was long and uncomfortable, but I hoped that it would never end. I knew what was waiting for me. I book in at the hotel 'Viel Gluck' in Hamelin. It is eerie to be in the town where it all started. I freshen up and go down to the hotel bar. A few couples and a family are dotted around.

"Fraulein? Bitte?"

I look at the bartender. "A glass of Hock, please."

The hotel owner, Karsten Bader, is socialising with his guests. I recognise him from the hotel's website. He is a large man with ruddy cheeks and a thick handlebar moustache. He works his way around the room, then approaches me.

"Guten Tag, fraulein. Wie sind Sie?"

"I'm sorry, I don't speak German," I reply.

"That is OK, fraulein," he booms, his face widening with the beginning of a broad smile, "nor do I."

We talk for a while. I am completely at ease with this kind man. The amount of wine I have drunk helps this feeling. During a rare lull in the conversation I ask my question. "Where did The Piper disappear with all those children?"

Karsten stares at me intently. He then looks away. "Jean, I like you. You're a nice lady. Some things you should not mention here. Although it happened a long time ago, we still remember. Descendants of the families that lost loved ones still live here. I am one. Please excuse me. I have to start closing up."

Shame-faced and drunk, I return to my room.

A noise in my room rouses me. A glance at the bedside clock. Two in the morning. I put on my glasses and peer harder into the gloom. There is a figure in the corner. I reach for the knife under my pillow. I am not scared. I am ready for him. The shape moves closer. I flick on the light. I spring out of the bed and stand there with my knife hand extended. It is not The Piper. I see an old man. He is leaning to one side on a crutch. He is small in stature, not much bigger than a child. He wears a ragged night shirt which, once white, is now filthy grey.

"What do you want?" I hiss at him.

"Put your knife away. I'm not here to harm you."

Although the figure is a pitiful sight, I still keep hold of the knife.

"You are looking for The Piper. I can help you," says the man. "I know where he is."

This information takes me a while to digest. "Where is he?" I gasp.

"I will take you there tomorrow. Meet me at the city gates 12 o'clock. Prepare for a long walk."

The man retreats to the corner of the room. Many questions vie for room in my head. "How do you know where he is?" I blurt.

"You are not the only one he has cursed," replies the man, angrily. "I have been lame from birth. When he took my friends, I couldn't keep up with them. They disappeared into the mountain. He damned me with eternal life."

I sit on the bed, shocked. The figure disappears.

From the city gates we cross the Weser River and make our way to the mountains. The fresh air washes over me like a rebirthing. The chatter of the birds is soothing. For a moment, I am at peace. My companion is not only taciturn but moves very fast. He speaks once to give his name, Ansell. Occasionally he turns to point the way. I feel great sorrow for this child. He has lived for hundreds of years in solitude with regret for his only friend. He must desire vengeance as much as I do.

When we finally stop the sun is setting over the mountains. The beauty of the sunset is in stark contrast to the horror we have to face. "This is it, fraulein," says Ansell. "This is where my friends entered the mountain."

I look at a solid rock face. I walk down an avenue of trees and join my friend. There is no discernible entrance.

Ansell has read my mind. "I have searched for many years for an entrance," he says, with a resigned sadness.

I consider the situation for a moment. What brought The Piper to me in the first instance? I start to shout. "Hello, you evil little man! Still persecuting children? Show yourself. Let us see the pathetic piper!"

I barely finish when I hear the grating noise of rough stone moving against rough stone. Ansell and I both hold our ears. The cacophony is too painful. We both scream and fall to the ground. Just when I think that my head will split open, it stops. We stand and brush dust and leaves off our clothes. A loud cough pervades the air. We turn and see that the rock face has opened. Standing in the entrance is The Piper.

He has not changed. The same face and form. We stand and stare at each other, like two gunslingers in the dusk. Ansell moves forward.

"Where are my friends?" he asks, his voice full of hurt.

The Piper moves to one side and gestures for Ansell to enter. Cautiously Ansell advances. When he reaches The Piper he edges along the rock, keeping as much distance as he can between himself and the creature. Ansell moves from the fading light and into the dark.

As the cave envelops him completely Ansell, the last of the Children of Hamelin, turns to dust.

I approach my nemesis. I feel the knife in my pocket. My gaze never leaves his. I get to within arm's length of him. I bring out the knife and flick it open. I lunge at him with all that I have. The Piper grips my wrist and twists. The pain is sharp. I drop the knife.

"Go on then, you bastard," I spit at him. "Finish it. My life has meant nothing since you came into it. Kill me."

He pulls me to him. I can smell his fetid breath. Then his lips are pressed against mine. His raspy tongue darts into my mouth. I try to resist. He is too strong.

After an age he releases me. He stands aside. I peer into the cave. I see Ansell's robe and crutch on the floor. Peace at last. Then I hear voices. "Miss! Miss! You've come back for us. We knew you would."

My children, the children The Piper stole from me in the classroom all those years ago, stand in the darkness. I rush to them and they surround me. I laugh and cry. The cave closes behind me. I do not care. I have a life again.

After the greetings have finished, I look round. The cave is illuminated by strands of phosphorous in the walls. I strain to see in the darkness. Where has he gone? Is he going to play one more trick to ruin my happiness? Near to Ansell's robe I see more rags. As I get closer to them, they become familiar. They are The Piper's garments. A small flute has been left on top of the pile. The Piper is nowhere to be seen.

FOR THE LOVE OF MOTHER

Paul Heywood, noted solicitor and friend to the stars, was in turmoil. Paul, nicknamed by the press as Paul 'Getsemoff' Heywood, was a very despondent man. His mother had just passed away. His mother who had brought him up on her own, his mother who had worked all the hours God sends to put him through the finest education available, his mother who had made him the man he was today. Heywood had spent a fortune in care and remedies to save her from the ravages of the terrible Alzheimer's disease. He had an annexe built on to his mansion near to the Surrey Green Belt, especially customized to cater for her every need. Around the clock supervision by carefully selected staff. He knew the end was coming for his beloved mother, but could not accept its finality.

She was buried, by special permission of the local council, at the very end of Heywood's immense garden. A traditional yew tree was planted adjacent to the site. Much to the chagrin of Heywood's wife, Fiona, he adorned the grave with a large headstone which sat on the right side of good taste. After the graveside service, everyone retired to the house for refreshments. Footballers, actors, councilmen and the odd relative that had not been alienated, went inside. Oblivious to everything around, Heywood remained by his mother's side, crippled by his loss. He shed tears that were never spared for victims of his many court victories, or for injustices over which he had presided. This man of means was reduced to a shell.

"Mr Heywood?"

He looked around, sharply. The voice had come from a petite old woman, who had crept up on him and was standing a few yards away. For a moment he saw his mother and was filled with glorious hope.

"Mother!" he cried out absurdly.

"No, Mr Heywood. I'm sorry. I'm not your mother," replied the old woman in a restrained whisper.

"Oh. I'm sorry," he replied, hope swiftly crushed.

The figure approached. Heywood almost stepped back as he regained focus through teary eyes. Her face resembled the hide of an elephant. Deep, deep creases sat indiscriminately across her entire face, criss-crossing where they warped around her features. These crevices provided the only colour on a gaunt, sallow visage. She smiled and displayed the few teeth that she had left, all yellow and brown from years of nicotine abuse. One feature looked quite out of place. Her hazel eyes were beautiful. They shone with sincerity, love. With hope.

"Please excuse this intrusion but I read about your mother in the local paper and came to pay my respects. I have met her on occasion in the village. She was a wonderful woman," the woman whispered, her voice raw and strained from heavy smoking.

"Yes, yes. She was," replied Heywood. "Would you like to join us for some food, or perhaps a drink?"

"No, thank you. I also came here to give you this. Please consider it. It may help your pain." The woman handed Heywood a flyblown card.

ARE YOU RECENTLY BEREAVED? ARE
YOU HAVING TROUBLE COPING?

THEN PLEASE TRY OUR SEANCE
SERVICE. PRIVATE SESSIONS, UTTER
DISCRETION GUARANTEED.

FIRST SITTING FREE, FEE ONLY APPLICABLE
ON COMPLETE SATISFACTION.

CALL US ON 00053876213.

BE WITH A LOVED ONE AGAIN.

Heywood looked up to speak to the woman, but she was already disappearing up the garden. He fingered the card thoughtfully and then placed it in his breast pocket.

There were several factors that lead to Heywood calling the number on the card. He was still in deep pain and this meeting might just ease the ache. He was always ready to try a new experience, however ridiculous it may seem. Finally, if these people tried to scam him then he could easily crush them with his power, wealth and expertise. So it was that Paul Heywood found himself in the living room of a modest house situated just outside the local village. The room was not how he had imagined it, his expectation having been corrupted by scenes of seances on film and television. The room was very modern in appearance. The suite was white leather, two large settees faced each other across a smoky glass coffee table. The few ornaments gave the room a minimalistic quality.

Beyond the settees was a circular glass dining table with six chrome and faux leather seats of an unusual design. Sitting in three of these chairs was an old man and a younger couple. The old woman he had met at the funeral stepped in front of him. "This way, Mr Heywood. We'll get started," she said encouragingly. Heywood sat next to one of the younger pair, leaving a spare seat between him and the old man. This was soon occupied by the old woman, much to the consternation of Heywood, who still found her repulsive.

"Mr Heywood, let me introduce you to the group. These young people are Susan and David Myers, recently married. The gentleman over there is Mr Samuel Watts, who is the main contact with the spirit world. Susan and David help us, as we helped them contact a lost one." The couple smiled and nodded as if to confirm what the old woman had said.

"And you are?" said Heywood to the old woman.

"Oh. I'm sorry. I haven't introduced myself. I'm Margaret Watts, Samuel's sister."

The old man, who had been staring at the ceiling since Heywood's arrival now looked at the table. "Let us begin," he said in a voice as soft as his sister's.

Heywood was encouraged to copy the younger couple and move around the table. All hands were then placed palm down on the surface with little fingers touching their neighbour's hand. Samuel looked up and then slumped in his seat as if asleep. It seemed like an eternity to Heywood until he heard a slight noise. As it grew in volume, the noise resembled the scratching noise an old record might make rotating under an uncaring needle. Heywood was not a man who was easily frightened but he felt himself tense in his seat as a voice knitted into the din.

"Where am I?" said the voice. It was the cry of a young child. "Where is my mummy?" the voice wailed in distress.

"Child, we want to speak to the spirit of Rose Heywood," said Samuel in a commanding voice.

"I want my *mummy*!" the child replied, screaming out the last word. Heywood cried out in a startled fear and the atmosphere around the table changed into an icy air, creating an atmosphere of great unease. Heywood was now completely entranced by the events. Through the next few minutes, he heard an assortment of voices, some asking questions that Samuel replied to. Samuel's head began to sag and his eyelids briefly closed.

"Enough!" shouted Samuel finally.

The room fell into silence. Heywood looked at Margaret Watts. "I'm afraid that is all for today," she said. "My brother is quite exhausted."

Heywood was obviously disappointed but still optimistic about further meetings on the strength of that afternoon's events. He made a further appointment with Margaret and left.

That first seance had lifted Heywood out of the mire of self-pity. He was now very confident about contacting his mother. Four days later on a dark Saturday evening, he found himself with the same group of people. The seance took the same form as the previous one. More voices, more questions, no Mother. Heywood was beginning to lose heart and patience when a voice, clearer in tone than the others, made him sit upright in his chair.

"Paul! Paul! Help me. Please help me. They are going to hurt me," came the cry of a woman in deep throes of panic. Heywood became very confused. He knew the voice, but it was not his mother's.

"Fiona? Fiona! That's my wife's voice," he said looking around the group in bewilderment. "What the hell is going on?"

Margaret Watts answered him. "A couple of our friends have visited your mansion, Paul. They've gone to retrieve a little compensation that was denied them by your slippery courtroom skills."

Heywood tried to get up, but the young man was behind him now, restraining him with a hand on his shoulder. Heywood could also feel the chill of a rigid, metal barrel against his cheek.

"You're clever enough to have worked out what's happened, aren't you, Paul," continued Margaret Watts. "At our first meeting our friends were studying your property. Now they are inside and having a jolly time, by all accounts. All the voices you've heard were obviously recordings, set up by us so that Samuel could reply accurately except the last one. That is your wife on a mobile phone. Shall we put her out of her misery?"

"NO!" cried Heywood almost simultaneously with the sound of the discharged bullet that ended the life of Fiona Heywood.

"You have made too many enemies and destroyed too many lives, Paul," said Margaret. "You came to us to contact your mother. Well we are going to grant that wish."

Paul 'Getsemoff' Heywood felt the end of the barrel against the back of his head. The only person he couldn't get off would be himself.

WHAT THE CAT SAW

The back door slammed. "Bloody hell!"

"Are you all right, Roger?" I said, "How was the gardening?"

"That bloody cat has crapped again, all over the lawn."

I smiled to myself. This was not a new occurrence.

"I swear, Nigel, if I get hold of that creature, I will throttle it."

"What, and leave that dear old lady without a friend? You're worse than the cat."

Roger laughed. "I don't crap everywhere. Anyway, what does that old bag do all day? We never see her. She makes all that racket next door. Banging away with her music blaring out. We don't even know her name, Nigel."

It was true. I had only ever seen her out at night, pulling a tartan shopping trolley with her cat's head poking out the top. When I shouted out to her, she didn't even look up.

"Perhaps you could take it to your surgery, Nigel. Do you still practise vivisection?"

I gave Roger a stern look. Having dedicated my life to the care of animals, 'vivisection' was not a word that I cared for.

"Sorry, Nigel," said Roger. "I would like to know what goes on in that house. We're working on some new hardware at work. Surveillance equipment for the military. I can 'borrow' some. I have full security clearance and it wouldn't be away too long. We could trap that cat and attach the bugs to it."

"Great Roger, where are you going to stick the cameras?"

"Up its arse and teach it to walk backwards."

"Charming."

"I'll fix the bugs to its collar. I know it has one. I've chased the bloody thing often enough."

"The old bat might be ancient. but I think she'd notice something on moggy's collar."

"For fuck's sake, Nigel. Why don't you come up with something instead of pissing on my parade?"

Roger looked to the ceiling, his forehead furrowed. I closed my eyes and thought.

"Bingo," I said. "We'll take the collar off the cat and give it a posh, new one with the equipment on it. We'll take it back to Miss Marple and tell her that we found the cat trapped in a fence, collar missing. I've had a delivery of new collars and I've got some samples here. I can supply her one from the goodness of my rich heart. She'll take Sir Crapsalot back and you do your magic on the computer. Then we'll see how many dead people she keeps in her lounge."

"Brilliant, Nigel, if she doesn't fall for it, we'll take the collar back and think on."

***

We caught the cat in our garden with the help of a tin of tuna and a large washing basket. Collar removed, we went to put the plan into action. Roger was carrying the cat, but he placed it on the floor still in his grasp. There was an agonised meow as he stepped on one of the cat's paws. I was angry at this sudden development and was about to tell him so.

"Just a small injury to make it look realistic and the old gal might not pay too much attention to the collar if fleabag is hurt," he said.

After an eternity of knocking on her door and shouting out that we had her pet, the old woman opened the door. The security chain was still on and all we could see was a grey, icy eyeball.

"What do you want?" she said. Her voice was so stern that we both jumped in unison.

"I think your cat's been in an accident," said Roger. "We found it outside on the pavement. It was limping quite badly - "

In an instance the door was opened, and the woman had grabbed hold of the cat. As I had never seen her clearly, I'd had preconceptions of what she would look like. Small, hunched over with a cracked face and drool dripping from thin lips. This woman was handsome. She had high cheekbones adorning a remarkably wrinkle-free face that was just on the wrong side of thin. She must have been five feet 11 inches tall and she stood erect like a schoolmistress patrolling the class looking for the first sign of misbehaviour. I realised then that I had judged her to be witch-like, haggard, badly dressed, smelly. I was ashamed.

"Where's his collar?" she snapped at us.

"Didn't know that he had one. That's how we found him. He has hurt his right, front paw. He was limping," said Roger.

"I'm a vet and I have some top of the range collars like the one he's wearing," I said. My bladder loosened as she pierced my mind with her cold eyes. "Those three buttons on the collar are de-wormers, a de-fleaer and a tracking device so that if your cat gets lost, we can trace it from the surgery."

There was a terrible silence. I could hear Roger's Adam's apple going up and down like a noisy lift. The woman glared at us both several times. The game was up...

The woman shut her front door with such force I stepped back, thinking that it would hit me. We heard chains and bolts being secured.

Roger was smiling. "Got her," he said. "Now let's go and do that voodoo that I do so well."

***

We sat our kitchen table where Roger had set up a computer which would relate images of the surveillance device from the cat. The buttons either side this were audio receptors. The computer screen came to life.

"Here, Tiddles, dinner time," said the woman and we watched as a bowl of food was placed in front of the cat.

Roger laughed out loud. "Tiddles? The way she looked I thought she would have could him Himmler or Goebbels," he said.

We watched Tiddles eating.

"Well this is exciting," I said. "If anything remotely interesting happens, do wake me up." And off to bed I went.

***

"Nigel! Nigel!"

I struggled to open an eye. Roger's silhouette leaned over me. I turned over, pulling the quilt with me.

"She's gone out. Come and have a look."

The picture on the screen was hazy. It improved as the old lady and her cat passed under a lamppost. The cat was sat in a small wicker trolley on wheels being pulled by his owner. The picture faded.

"I'll just switch to night vision," said Roger.

The scene improved dramatically. "What you computer nerds can't do," I said in admiration.

The old lady was walking down a street that was unfamiliar to us. It was a narrow road guarded on either side by terraced housing. The old lady stopped in front of one house. Pulling her trolley behind her, she walked up to the front door. She knocked.

A light came on. The door opened. The opening was almost filled by the shape of a large man. He looked at the old lady.

"It's a bit late to be collecting for the Red Cross, deary," he said.

There was a sound of the wind rushing quickly through a small pipe. A dot appeared on the man's forehead. Something trickled out of it. The man crumpled to the floor.

"Bloody hell, Nigel," said Roger, incredulously, "she's shot him."

****

I was pacing up and down the living room rubbing my forehead until it hurt.

"What the hell are we going to do?" said Roger.

"We are going to tell the police what we saw," I replied.

"What are we going to tell them, Nigel? That we thought it was a jolly wheeze to kidnap a cat? That it was a jape to illegally fit stolen, classified surveillance equipment to it? We'd lose our jobs. I'd go to prison."

"We need to get the camera back. Wipe the computer memory. Then forget what we saw."

"Then we'll get the hell out of this area. Agreed?"

"Agreed."

***

We put on our thinking caps once more and the next day the old lady received a note. Cannibalised from newspaper headlines, it read:

> I KNOW ABOUT YOUR NOCTURNAL
> ACTIVITIES. MEET ME AT THE
> FOUNTAIN IN WALMSLEY
> PARK AT 2000HRS TONIGHT.
> COME ALONE. UNARMED.

We had never seen the woman in a car and were certain that she didn't possess one. Walmsley Park was a two-hour journey by bus, there and back. The old lady might wait half an hour until she realised that no-one is coming. That was plenty of time to get the cat, remove the webcam. The problem was that the cat didn't want to be caught.

"We have been crouched outside this flap for 20 minutes, Roger. He's not falling for it again."

Roger was knelt by the cat-flap. In his hand was a plate of tuna chunks. I couldn't help laughing as he called 'Tiddles' continuously.

"What do you suggest we do then, Professor?" replied an irritated Roger.

"We may not get this opportunity again," I said. "We'll have to break in."

For a murderer, the old lady wasn't very careful. We eased open a rear sash window. Roger went first. I followed through the window, into the kitchen. We heard a hiss and then 'meow'. The cat darted out of the kitchen into the hallway and disappeared through an open door. We approached the door.

"Hurry up, Nigel, or we'll lose the bloody thing," said Roger.

We stood in the entrance to the door. It led down to a basement room. The first thing I noticed was the smell. Not dank or musty but a clean smell like a hospital ward. Bleach and cleaning fluid but mixed with the smell of WD40. I felt along the wall and found the light switch.

There was a wooden table which took up the entire length of the far wall. There was a variety of hand tools hanging in neat rows on the wall above the table. Varying sizes of hammers, screwdrivers, saws all in line. Small cleaning brushes, like the type used to clean babies' bottles, were standing in a glass jars on the table. They were covered in oil. Rags, WD40, even a microscope adorned the surface of the table. "What do you think this is?" said Roger. He was holding a small, metallic tube. At one end there was a smaller tube attached. It was highly polished and sparkled like black diamond under the light.

I took it. "Jesus Christ!" I exclaimed. "This is a silencer for a gun."

"Let's get out of here, Nigel," said a worried Roger. "She'll be ages yet. We still need to get that cat."

**

As we searched, the basement gave up more surprises. Targets in the form of human torsos hung from the ceiling. Locked metal cabinets of various sizes. A wall covered in newspaper articles, all relating to murders. Some of the clippings dated from a long time ago. One corner of the room was decorated with white tiles. Floor to ceiling, emanating out into the room. Some of the tiles had been badly cracked. In places the grouting was a very dark red.

"I think she shoots people in here, Nigel."

"You are a clever, young man, aren't you?" The old lady had crept up behind us. She held a gun. "You two must think that I am a very foolish old woman. Nobody gives anything for free least of all hi-tech surveillance which I discovered with my microscope, some delicate tools and a steady hand. I thought that someone would come back to retrieve it when they uncovered my 'occupation'. Here you are."

I was rooted to the floor. It was extraordinary to see this thin, grey-haired woman grasping a gun that looked too heavy for her to hold.

"We know what you're up to. We've called the police," said Roger, his voice sounding unconvincing.

The old lady smirked at him. She held us at gun-point for a minute as if she was undecided what to do with us. Then her shoulders slumped. She lowered her gun hand. She sighed.

"I get tired of this world. So much wrong. I try my best to clean up the streets. For every scumbag I dispose of another two come along. I will never stop, though. Someone has to hold back the tide."

The old lady raised her gun. She shot Roger. Middle of his forehead. Dead.

Tears of shock and rage cascaded down my face. "Why? Why, you sick bitch?"

The old lady went to a three-drawer filing cabinet. She opened the top drawer and muttered to herself as she flicked through the files.

"Brackley, Bracknall. Here we are, Braddock, Roger." She took out a beige paper folder. She threw it to me.

The first page in the file was an A4 picture of Roger. I flicked through the rest of the documents.

Previous convictions. Addresses for home and work. His daily routine. His whole life.

"A client did not take kindly to your friend, or more precisely, what he kept on his computer," said the old woman. "This was going to be a difficult assignment with you living next door. You made it much easier for me. Thank you."

I let the file slip to the floor. I turned and started walking up the stairs.

"Don't forget," said the old lady. I looked at her. She was waving her gun at me. "Just you be a good boy. Don't forget, a cat has nine lives. You don't."

ONE IN FOUR

Don't care
Can't care
Won't care

Don't comprehend
Can't comprehend
Won't comprehend

I'll get a grip on my life
I'll pull myself together
I'll think of those worse off than me
Thank you for the guilt trips
I'll keep them in mind
While I decide
To live or die

Don't ring
Can't ring
Won't ring

Don't visit
Can't visit
Won't visit

I'm not contagious
Despite what you've heard
You will not be tainted
By my disease
If any of the above applies
Damn you
From a one in four

THE ROSES OF WAR

INTERNAL INVESTIGATION (O.I.C. MAJOR THOMAS TINDALL)

SUB. H.Q. DELTA, SARISBURY PLAIN

TRANSCRIPT OF VIDEO RECORDING

SUBJECT: PAUL EVANS (CIVILIAN)

LOCATION: FLAT 1, 52, MEGSON AVENUE, SARISBURY

DATE OF RECORDING: 7TH JULY, 2020

COMMENCE.

My name is Paul Evans. I don't know if anyone will pick up this message, I don't know if anybody else is still alive. I'm goin' to tell this story as well as I can, I'm not very good with words, not like my missus, Jan [SOBBING]. She's brainier than me but... [RECORDER PANS LEFT TO DECEASED FEMALE IDENTIFIED AS JAN EVANS, SUBJECT'S SPOUSE, SAT ON SETTEE ADJACENT TO SUBJECT.] You see. You see that bloody, stupid, plastic flower in her hands, that's what killed her. I'll try and remember what happened, I might guess at some things, but here goes.

These roses started poppin' up everywhere. Last Christmas, I think. Given away for nothin' in shops, pubs, with newspapers and mags [MAGAZINES]. They were free so people lapped 'em up. They also had a little label on 'em, the name of some plastics firm, Rosedell, Roswell, something like that. There was also a promise that for every rose given out, £1 would be given to charity. You had to text or e-mail a number with how many you 'ad, your postcode and the name of a charity and Bob's your uncle. This firm even claimed on posters that one million pounds had already been given to a charity for good will. They also said that when ten million had been given out then the charity money would start pourin' in. As far as I know everyone, from MPs to street cleaners, were taken in. Even Jan, who hates clutter, brought a couple home and put 'em in an old vase, they didn't look too bad [SOBBING].

It all calmed down after a few weeks, but the roses were still available and wherever you went there they were, homes, pubs, hospitals even the local nick. Then things began to happen, strange things. I read in the paper that some journo [JOURNALIST] had tracked down the plastics factory in the middle of nowhere, but couldn't contact anyone there, didn't even see anyone there. All she heard was machines working away.

She also found out that the charity this firm had claimed to have given a million quid to was made up, didn't exist. Some people thought, "Bloody journos, always poking their noses in where they're not wanted. Christ! It was for charity." I know I did. Soon after I read this, I read that this journo had copped it.

She was walking home when someone came up to her, twisted her head and broke her neck. Broke her bleedin' neck! Broad daylight, I mean it must have been around Easter 'cause I remember those flowers appearing with eggs and on hats and that. I read that the killer wasn't too careful either. Plenty of witnesses who saw the murder and then saw the murderer just vanish into air, gone. Respectable people as well you know, no idiots. Big investigation, TV, papers, appeals. No joy.

Not long after was when all the unexplained deaths 'appened. People just dropping dead. Hundreds and then thousands. Hospitals and the police were overrun, but they were dyin' too. More and more bodies in the streets, in their homes, even a whole pub in Doncaster I heard on the radio. The government organised a 'Thinktank', whatever that was. Then real sudden like they said that it was the flowers, the damn roses. They said that as it got warmer the roses gave off some kind of gas which would kill you. 'Course people started to throw them out in panic, but that just left them to spread the gas in the street, killin' more. Jan was about to get rid of ours when the bloody things went off. She gasped, fell back onto the sofa and died. I tried to help her, but I had this great pain through my body. My guts felt like they were being used for football practise, I was so sick for days and did think I was goin' to snuff it, but I didn't, I survived. I wish I hadn't.

There were other attacks reported by the government. Same as the journo, folk were having their necks broken, but whoever did it was invisible. No-one saw nothin', just out of the blue people dyin' and not knowing who was doin' it or when it was comin. That's why I've stayed indoors. I'm really scared. I don't want to end up like all those people and that journo. Hang on. That journo was killed by a man who vanished.

Christ! I see it now. Not only are they invisible but they can change into us. They could be anyone, anywhere.

Christ! Invisible or human...

[RECORDING PAUSED FOR
9 MINUTES, 22 SECONDS.]

[RECOMMENCED.]

I am really, really scared and alone. I don't know what to do. Just sat here waiting for death. If someone knocks on the door, it could be one of them, what should I do? I hope this recording gets picked up and helps someone to survive and also -

[SOUND OF FRONT DOOR BEING FORCED.]

EVANS: Who's there?

MARINE A [COVERING SUBJECT WITH MACHINE GUN]: Put your hands in the air, now!

EVANS: All right! OK!

MARINE B: She's dead and he's alive. He must be one of those things.

EVANS: No. I'm human. I survived.

MARINE A: Don't trust him. He has got to be hiding in human form.

EVANS: No. Feel me. I'm human.

MARINE B: Stay back! Get on the floor!

[WEAPON DISCHARGE.]

MARINE A: He's bleeding. I think he was human.

MARINE B: Christ what have I done? I thought he was going to- Wait. Turn that bloody camera off!

END OF TRANSCRIPT

PLAYING BOARD GAMES
WITH UNCLE FRANK

"Morning, Dad," I said. I was late. Just enough time for a piece of toast.

"You stupid little cow!" he shouted back. The palm of his hand hit the target. My cheek throbbed painfully. My eyes watered.

"What the hell was that for?"

He picked up a board and threw it on to the table. It knocked his tea over.

"You've been going through my room again," I said. The board on the table was mine. I got it as a present from someone very close to me.

"Just as well. What are you playing at?"

Mum came into the kitchen. "What's all the shouting about, Bob?" she said. Dad pointed at the board. Mum picked it up. "O-O-J-A-Y board?" she read out loud.

"No, Janet. It's pronounced W-E-J-Y-A," replied Dad.

"What's it for, Bob? What is the alphabet and all those numbers at the bottom doing on it?"

"It's one of those boards kids use. They try to talk to the dead. Or summon evil spirits. Bloody dangerous, if you ask me."

"Where have I seen one before?" said Mum. She was still puzzled.

"That horror film we saw in the 70s. Where the little girl plays with a Ouija board. Then she starts behaving badly. She pukes over a vicar. Turns her head right round, by herself. What was the name of that film?" asked Dad.

"*The Exorcist*, Dad," I replied, "And I don't use the board like that."

I shrunk as his hand raised again.

"Better get off to school, Cathy, before I give you a bloody good hiding and give your dad a rest," said Mum, pushing me roughly out of the kitchen.

"We'll talk about this when you get home tonight," Dad yelled at me as I closed the front door.

***

It took several attempts before my shaking hand fitted the key into the front door. I walked slowly inside. I was expecting one type of attack or another: verbal or physical.

"Cathy," called Mum. "Come upstairs to your bedroom."

My heart emptied. My bladder filled. I trudged up the stairs.

My room was gloomy. The curtains had been pulled. The only light shone from several randomly placed candles. Mum and Dad were sat in front of me, between my bed and the wardrobe. As I moved closer, I saw that they had set up my Ouija board on a small table.

"Your mum and me have been busy researching this afternoon. We are going to show you just how risky playing with this board is. Sit on your bed and watch," said Dad.

I slumped onto my bed. Using two fingers each, they pushed a small glass around the board. After the glass slid to several letters on the board, Dad said out loud what the glass had just spelled out. "Is anybody there?"

The glass slid to 'YES' on the board.

"Are you the devil?"

The glass indicated 'YES'.

"Show yourself."

Nothing happened.

"Show yourself, now!" shouted Dad.

My bedroom door flung open and the light from the hallway silhouetted a figure in the doorway. It slowly came forward. It had to stoop to enter the room, because this apparition had two large horns protruding from the top of the head. It stopped in front of Mum and Dad. The face of this creature was bright red. It had an ebony black moustache with goatee beard. Its eyes were cat-like, yellow with a thin black stripe. It was bare-chested. Underneath two medallions that adorned the chest was a reversed pentagram. It was drawn in red with small red trails weaving down to give the effect of blood. It was wearing leather trousers and knee-high boots. I could see the end of a tail through its legs.

"What do you want?" said Dad. He was standing in front of Mum. He had his fists clenched and raised. The creature turned slowly. It was now facing me. It raised an arm. It pointed at me.

My eyes were wide. Tears had started to make their way down my cheeks. I couldn't take it any longer. I erupted with laughter. Pain shot down my sides. I genuinely feared that I would wet my bed.

"What's so bloody funny?" asked Dad. I looked up at him through blurred, watery eyes. He was not happy.

"Was this supposed to scare me?" I said, struggling to compose myself. "Firstly, nobody says 'is anybody there?' on a Ouija board anymore. That is so last century. I can see how you slid the glass along. The board is covered in cooking oil."

I waited for these revelations to register. I then went for the coup de grace.

"And finally, a big 'up' for our devil. How's it going, Uncle Frank? I knew it was you. That is the same costume you wore last Halloween. You are the only bloke I know who wears a crucifix and a St. Christopher chain. And, finally, the hairless chest and appendix scar. You need to work on your devil costume."

Uncle Frank ripped off his mask. He gave me an embarrassed grin. He started to laugh. "Sorry, kid. They promised me a shit-load of beer for taking part in this little charade. I knew you'd rumble it."

"It's OK, Uncle Frank. Gave me a good laugh, too." I replied.

That was too much for Dad. He clambered onto my bed. The first blow was into my stomach and not only took my breath away but made me wretch. I could feel my face redden and cut as fists rained down on me. It felt as like someone was cutting my face and then hitting it with a small but powerful hammer. My vision blurred. I thought I was going to die.

Uncle Frank dragged Dad off me and ushered him out. "That's enough, Bob. For God's sake."

Mum stood there, staring down at me. "You deserved that, you snide little bitch. You can stay up here. I don't want to see you. Not even for dinner."

A picture fell off the wall as the door slammed shut.

"Who the hell is it?" shouted Dad in response to my boisterous knocking on his bedroom door.

I opened the door. I stood there in silence while bedside lamps were switched on.

"Cathy! What the bloody hell do you want?" said Mum.

"I've brought someone to see you," I replied.

I stood aside. Our guest entered the bedroom. There were twin gasps from Mum and Dad.

A metal garment, worn as a nappy, was the only article of clothing on this creature. It was fixed to the torso with nails that ran through the top of the device. The nails then pierced the creature's body. Multiple wounds of every shape and size punctuated his entire frame, front and back. The wounds were open, and blood ran from each wound. The blood did not fall onto the floor. The blood from each wound ran into a different wound, like a gruesome recycling process. The creature had two faces. His eyes were dark red, with no white showing. He didn't have any noses. His mouths were large, open orifices, totally dark inside, contorted in agony. The creature had no hair. The two faces were connected with thick bands of scar tissue as if they had been welded together.

Mum had the quilt up to her eyes. Her eyes had grown wide with fear. I looked at Dad. His eyes had narrowed. His brow creased. A sudden realisation came to him.

"Is that you, Frank?" he timidly asked. The creature did not answer.

"Janet. That's Frank in fancy dress again," Dad said, turning to Mum. Mum dropped the quilt.

"Frank, you silly sod," she said. "Do you know what time it is? As for you, young lady. You've just added to all the trouble you're already in."

"Shut up, Bob and Janet," I yelled. "You think this wretched creature is Uncle Frank? Who's this, then?"

Uncle Frank looked over my shoulder. He gave a cheery wave. "Hello, Bob. Hello, Janet," he said.

Mum and Dad's jaws dropped open in unison. Their eyes turned from Frank back to our visitor. "Who is this?" whispered Dad.

I took a moment to relish this situation, before speaking. "Uncle Frank and I made a little call on the Ouija board this evening. This is Rymise. He is a demon from ancient Babylonian culture. He is said to have endured every pain and suffering caused by mankind. In revenge, when summoned, he will inflict pain and suffering on chosen victims. Congratulations. Uncle Frank and I selected you."

Uncle Frank and I backed out of the bedroom as Rymise stepped towards Bob and Janet. The door closed independently. As we walked downstairs, we could hear the screaming start. I looked at Uncle Frank.

"Thanks, Uncle, for all your help. And for teaching me the ways of the Ouija board."

"That's OK, kiddo. Now, is there anyone else hurting you?"

THE GIRL IN MY MIRROR

I was cleaning my teeth one morning, trying to get rid of the smell of scotch before I went to work, when something peculiar happened. Looking into my bath-room mirror, I saw the reflection of a woman staring back at me. Not my reflection but this beautiful girl. I splashed my face with cold water. Perhaps the booze was having fun with my brain. I looked back up. There she was. I grinned and she did the same. I poked out my tongue. She copied me. I could have continued but time was pressing. Maybe she'd be gone by tonight. I grabbed my keys and left the flat for work.

***

"Hell of a day," I said to myself as I slumped into a chair with a healthy slug of Scotland's finest. Suspended. They said that I was drunk again. Rubbish! I've been worse than that before and they haven't said anything. I didn't know that you had to be sober just to post a few letters and sort some mail. In any case, I didn't need that awful job. I decided to pop down to the local and cheer myself up. I went into the bathroom to have a shave and remembered the mirror incident from that morning. I looked tentatively into the mirror. There she was again. She was indeed beautiful. Golden blonde hair cut short into a bob, pronounced cheek bones that accentuated her eyes, which, in turn, were lit up by heavenly blue. Below her perfectly proportioned button nose was a full and sensual pair of lips, parted slightly in the centre to reveal the white of her teeth.

I knew this girl. I just couldn't place her. Was she someone I had delivered to? She didn't work in the sorting room, I knew that much. Even though I lived alone in my flat, I wasn't disturbed in any way about this occurrence. Drinking too much gives you all sorts of courage. Forgetting to shave, I turned to leave for the pub. Before I went, I had one last look in the mirror. She was still there, returning my smile. I hoped that she would be there when I came home.

The Stoat and Ferret was a dump. My little flat is not a palace but I do like to keep it clean when I'm able. I wouldn't bring a dog into this pub. Wallpaper peeled sorrowfully from the walls and the upholstery on the seats around them was split badly in places, exposing the foam interior. It was extensively stained, mainly with booze that had been spilled and left, in the vain hope that it would clean itself up. The carpet was the dark multi-patterned type that pubs prefer but in this case, you could not make out the pattern because of its filthiness. The many threadbare areas were perhaps its best feature. I settled on a bar stool and tried to catch someone's attention.

Being a Monday, the place was quite empty, which was good for me as I didn't really want to converse with any of the usual suspects. Attention on the beer pumps, I wasn't looking at the barmaid, but I knew she was there. Who else was going to pull my pint?

"Hello love, what are you after?" she asked.

"I'd like a-" the words stuck in my throat as I glanced up. There she was. The girl in my mirror. This is where I knew her. I normally leave here very inebriated. That is why I couldn't place her. I became wary that I was staring at her.

"I'm so sorry, you just reminded me of someone. I'll have a pint of your strongest guest ale," I blurted out. The transaction completed, I drank the warm, sweet beer down to half a pint and looked at the floor. I hoped that she had forgotten me instantly.

I couldn't forget her. I even left the pub early because I found myself staring at her like a starving man would look at a plate of food. Instead of returning straight home to end this state of sobriety, I walked the streets for a while. I walked amongst the litter and the dog mess. Past the graffiti that covered all available wall space with no art or design and declared: 'SHEILA IS A SLAG', 'CUM ON ARSENAL', 'KILL THE PEEDOS'. Past the bus-stop that had its windows broken once again, small shards of glass shining on the ground like diamonds that had lost their way. I no longer hated this place or this world, I have just become so disheartened with it all. It was at times like these I became very depressed. It felt as if my mind was closing down and the rest of my body was going to. My spirit and joie de vivre had already long gone. A profound dull feeling rose up from my cold heart to my bloodshot eyes. I needed to be numb again. I knew just the thing.

I woke up, next day in the afternoon on the couch. Everything was present and correct. The pain in my skull which seemed to cry out 'No more', the sour taste of staleness resting on my tongue, the translucent spots mocking me as they danced before my unfocused eyes. The telly was still on, although I hadn't a clue as to what I had been watching. Leaning forward to turn it to standby, my withered brain kicked my skull again in protest. I winced with the pain. You never get used to it. Then the weirdest thing happened. An image appeared on the shiny greyness of the telly. Looking closer, I could just about discern that it was the girl. The girl in the mirror, the girl in the pub. I rushed into the bathroom. There she was again, staring back at me. Where next? The bedroom where I barely slept. A forgotten mirror above the bed. Anxiously, I tiptoed into the bedroom and crawled across the bed until I was on all fours under the mirror. Very slowly, I raised myself up. I stifled a small groan of fear as the beautiful woman looked down on me.

"Don't run away from me, Frank," she said, her voice soft and pleading. That is just what I did. Collecting wallet and keys, I rushed out and headed for the one place where everything made sense.

Soon after, I was sitting on a bar stool in the Stoat and Ferret supplementing my pint with a whiskey chaser.

"You're early today, Frank," said Les, the landlord. "You all right?"

"Yeah, I'm fine," I lied, wishing he would leave me. He gave me a look that suggested he didn't believe me but didn't care. I moved away from the bar.

The sharpness of my mind was severely blunted by the time the girl arrived for her evening shift. She gave me a perfunctory smile and turned to serve one of the five other people who had stumbled across this slum. I looked at her through bleary eyes. I wanted her and she obviously wanted me from what she had said that morning. I could hold back no longer and the next time she passed by, I leant over and grabbed her by the arm.

"Why are you in my home?" I said to her, my words tripping over themselves and over my tongue.

"What are you on about?" she replied. She fixed me with a stare so severe that the Devil would have pissed himself. She tried to look bigger by hunching her shoulders and thrusting out her chest. Didn't work. She had nice boobs.

"You are in my home. You told me not to run away. Well I won't. You're lovely. Come out with me." The girl, this girl of my desires, started to shout. "Les! Les! Help me." I let go of her arm and tried to put my hand over her mouth.

"No. It's all right. I love you. I love you."

Les was a burly man with many years in the trade. I soon found myself on the pavement looking up at him.

"Frank, you'd better not come back in for a while. Sort yourself out, mate," he said with a modicum of concern and kindness. Struggling to my feet, I once again staggered home.

In addition to the pain, there was something else present the following afternoon. It was shame. Humiliation. That woman had turned me down flat. I felt the hatred and disgust flowing from her. Why, when she told me not to run away? Is she playing games with me? I could not comprehend this chain of events. I sat there questioning my very existence.

A noise from the bathroom. Laughter. I didn't expect to see that girl again after her brutal rejection. There she was. In my mirror. She was laughing. She was laughing a cruel, callous laugh. Worst still, she was laughing at me. Her gaze never left mine. I could take no more.

I smashed the mirror with my fist. Daggers fell to the ground, some red with my blood.

"Take that, you bitch," I said with an air of relief. It was over. No, it wasn't. More laughter. The television screen. I picked up the telly and threw it against the wall. Still, laughter pierced my mind. The bedroom. The last mirror was destroyed by my bloodied hand. I sank face forward into the welcoming quilt and buried my head as deep as I could into the fragrant cover. All around me was the sound of her laughter, echoing off the walls and ceilings and into the chaos of my mind. I must be rid of her. I knew what to do.

I left home around 11 o'clock that evening. The laughter eventually went as I sobered up during the day. I was shaking badly. I needed a drink. More than a drink, I needed a clear head. I walked the short distance to the Stoat and Ferret, avoiding eye contact with the few people I came across. I waited across the road from the pub and watched. I didn't wait long. Out came the girl. I pulled the hood of my top over my head. I let her walk for a short distance and then followed. My prayers were answered as she turned down an alleyway that ran behind a row of terraced houses. Breaking into a light jog, I caught up with her. She didn't hear me until it was too late. She turned just in time to see the heavy-duty spanner I had brought from home crash down onto her forehead. She fell. I set upon her with vigour, trying to exorcise the shame and anger within me. I didn't *mean* to kill her. When she lay motionless, I stopped with the spanner. I looked furtively around and, certain that I had not been seen, I ran home.

Once home, I took the drink that my body was aching for. My top and jeans were heavily blood-stained. I took no chances. Having changed, I took my bloody clothes to a nearby park. There, with the help of white spirit, I set fire to them. I threw the spanner far into the trees and bracken that surrounded the area. Job done, I returned home.

I slept well that night and for the first time in an eternity I woke up early and sober. I cleaned up the glass in the various rooms and dumped it in some-body's bin from the flats across the road. There was one task left. Taking the bus there and back, I bought a cheap bathroom cabinet from Argos. I had to know if that girl was out of my life. At home, I fixed the cabinet to the wall and then took out the mirror. Taking care not to look into it just yet, I placed it in position. Slowly, I closed the door to the cabinet. The mirror came into view. Broken, bruised and battered she looked back at me. Nose bent, eyes swollen, sensual lips split and bloodied, she gazed into my depths. No longer beautiful. Then she faded from view and I was left looking at my own pale and drawn features.

I was reinstated at work with a final warning as my punishment. I still drank too much but I was more careful now. I wanted to keep my job. The police did talk to me. I told them about the incident with the girl. I explained that I had a serious drink problem. I said how sorry I was about it. I also said that I was comatose at home when she was killed. There was nothing linking me to the murder, and they let me be. A poor old sop who didn't know the time of day. Then one day I was cleaning my teeth getting ready for work, when I looked into the mirror. Looking back at me was a gorgeous woman. I thought I knew her. I hope she is still there when I return from work. I am sure I'll see her somewhere and then... Well. Who knows what might happen?

SOUTHAMPTON
TO
ST IVES

I boarded the train at Southampton and sat down in the first class compartment. I was thankful that it was empty as I was too morose for company. I placed the urn on the table and studied it. The remains of a person. A life. Mary. I didn't want to make this journey but it was a promise made a long time ago. St Ives was the place she felt happiest. A time of calm, love, boundless sunshine, eternal joy. That was until Roger left. Then there was nothing. A barren chasm stretched before her. The return home. Friends that didn't care or didn't know how to care. Eventual abandonment. Death. She laid on her bed for two months before she was found. Empty pill bottles mirroring an empty life. I let a solitary tear run its course.

At some point, a ticket inspector approached. I searched my handbag for my ticket to no avail. I looked up to him in a blind panic. He had a kind, wizened face that put me at ease.

"I'm sorry, I can't find-"

"That is all right. I am not here for your ticket. I am here for you."

He sat down across from me. His uniform seemed old-fashioned, a buttoned-up tunic with faded gold braid on his trousers. While he appeared old, there was something youthful about him. He reminded me of a young actor playing a much senior role. His voice was melodic; it made me think of smooth chocolate being poured into my ear. "Are you sure you want to go to St Ives? Why don't you go back to Southampton and rest among friends and family?"

"I made a pledge years ago. Not just for her, but for the only man she ever loved. I'm going back to the place where she was the happiest."

The ticket inspector looked at me thoughtfully. I felt trapped by his piercing gaze. "Very well," he said with an air of reluctance. "Be warned that someone wants what you have. You are in considerable danger and I am unable to help you."

The inspector got up. "No. Wait," I replied, "I need to know who and why-"

At that precise moment, the compartment passed through a tunnel. The lights flickered temporarily. When they returned to normal, he was gone.

My blouse stuck to my back with the sweat of fear. I gasped as I realised I had stopped breathing. Should I get off and go back? What have I got that anyone would possibly want? The journey had become more difficult than it already was. I didn't see the man sit down opposite me. It seemed that he had appeared as suddenly as the inspector had vanished. He was beautiful. Lips of scarlet set into a marble jaw. Short, well-groomed stubble that spread to his chiselled cheekbones. Short, spiky hair so black it shone like ebony lit by a pale moonlight. His eyes were completely obscured by a stylish pair of dark sunglasses. He wore a black V-neck T-shirt and a long black leather trench coat. As he spoke to me in velvety tones, I found myself becoming attracted to this stranger. My chest heaved and my pulse became rapid.

"Hello, my dear. What an onerous journey you have undertaken. The burden must be great. Such responsibility. I can help."

Still captivated by him, I managed to splutter a reply. "How can you help? You don't know who I am, or even where I am going."

"Give me the urn," he said, leaning forward. "Your voyage will be at an end. You will be at peace."

Despite his seductive manner my vow was far too strong to hand him the urn. "I can't. I have to finish what I have begun."

The man's charming smile turned into a menacing grimace. In an instance, he was crouched on the table. I grasped the urn to my chest. "Silly girl," he hissed at me, "you cannot deny me. Give me that soul. You cannot dream of the agony that awaits you."

The man raked my hand with his fingernails. As they dragged across my skin, they left behind a searing pain. His nails were filthy, yellow claws, leaving deep cuts in their wake. He laughed as I screamed. "I want your soul, woman. Then you can be part of my sera-glio. Forever."

"You cannot have this one, Azael."

The man looked up as I looked around. At the far exit was another man. He was dressed in a long, light-tan leather coat. His head was adorned with flowing golden hair. He too was wearing sunglasses.

"And why not, Gabriel?" Azael replied, angrily.

Gabriel walked towards us. "There are two essences involved in this. They both rely on each other. I have orders that they be re-united."

Azael jumped down. I jumped up from my seat and moved away as the two men faced each other. The silence was eternal. Azael spoke first. "If I concede now, I demand the next beautiful soul."

Gabriel looked skyward and then turned to Azael. "It is done. Go back to your hole, Azael."

Azael let out a roar like a wounded behemoth. It shattered any object made of glass including all of the windows. This caused a wild maelstrom in the carriage. Table cloths desperately tried to cling on to their tables but were ripped into the air, and swirled like linen whirlwinds before crashing into the door. Glasses and cutlery chimed in unison, making strange music together as they raced for somewhere to rest. Azael transformed into a bull-like creature. His muscular form and the deep blackness of his coat made him look mountainous. Smoke bellowed from his nostrils and his horns pierced the roof of the carriage. Black wings grew in stages from his back until they too reached the ceiling. His eyes had become red lasers and they burned the back of my eyes. Azael turned to the exit. He was gone before he got there.

"Come here, Mary. Come, child." Still gripping the urn, I went to Gabriel. He offered his open arms. As I fell into his embrace, I was enveloped by his giant wings.

***

Gabriel opened his wings and released me. I stood on a rocky peninsular, staring out to sea. I knew where I was. St Ives Lighthouse was to my right. The sea, a savage beast, crashed against the rocks. The sound was as comforting as an old pair of slippers. I was overcome by a combination of despair and a heavy, grieving heartache mixed with elation and wonder. I noticed Gabriel stood by me.

"There is somebody here I think you know."

Turning around, I saw the ticket inspector stumbling towards me on the rocky carapace. As he approached, his features blurred and changed. By the time he reached me, he had fully transformed.

"Oh my God!" I yelled. It was Roger. My love. The happiest time of my life. I flung my arms around him, almost taking us down onto the stony floor. We kissed. It was yesterday.

Gabriel interrupted the re-union. "Before we go, you have one last task, Mary."

I knew what I had to do. I opened the urn and released my body to the sea below. It was the same place as I had released Roger's ashes so many years ago. We watched, Roger and I, as the briny deep took what remained of us on this world.

Gabriel said to me, "Your journey here on the train was part of your journey to the afterlife. I gave you, Mary, familiar surroundings to ease the transition.

Azael discovered my plan and tried to tempt you. You are both safe now. Let us complete your journey."

We felt the comfort of Gabriel's wings around us.

And then we were gone.

THE SYMPTOM OF
THE UNIVERSE

I've no idea where I am, but there is a soft pinkish light that is very soothing, comforting. I can hear a gentle, rhythmic beat. Ba-dum, ba-dum, ba-dum. Not only can I hear it, but I can also feel it. It could drive me insane if I stay here much longer, but where is here? I tentatively stretch out towards the delicate hue. The walls that surround me are cushioned, yielding but impenetrable. I can feel no way out. I am trapped. I must stay calm and breathe, gently breathe. Tired now, far too much exertion. Sleep.

I'm falling through the universe. I'm not scared. The stars that surround come closer. They flash before my eyes. They are not stars. They are knowledge, facts, data. I'm allowed a moment to absorb this information. Each star then recedes back into the Darkness, to be replaced by another.

This knowledge fills my head. Pythagorean theorem. Historical events. Dates. Conflict. Love. I am alive with the euphoria these facts have brought. I digest each word, every morsel.

Awake. It is very claustrophobic now. Claustrophobic. A funny word. Nice to say. Clostro-foe-bick. Warm glow. Ba-dum, ba-dum. I stretch out. The walls are getting closer. I push. The walls yield but come back even closer. I kick and punch. My efforts are futile. I tire. I fight against the tiredness. No use. Sleep.

I am looking down into a room. There is a woman lying on a bed. Next to her stands a man. They are holding hands. The woman looks in great discomfort. Her face contorts with pain from time to time. She occasionally screams, painfully. The man utters soothing words. He wipes the sweat from her forehead. This room has an aura. It is an aura of hope. Of love. I look closer. These people are very familiar to me. I sense a close connection between us. I think hard. I cannot remember.

Awake. The walls come nearer. I struggle, desperately. My cell again yields. It doesn't give. I begin to lose coherent thought. That nice word? Claustra? Clausto? I feel a small gap in my prison. It has opened above my head. I push hard and hope. I ascend. Then I become aware of the rope. It connects me to the cell. I am tied to the ever-closer walls. Will I ever be free?

I am easing through the gap. Noise. Bright light. I try to call out. My mind is blank. What is happening? Can't remember anything. I'm falling. My rope will save me. It gives. What is..? What..?

"Waaaaaaaaaaaah! Waaaaaaaaaaaaah!"

"Congratulations to the both of you. You have a beautiful baby girl."

THE THREE MUSICIANS
OF MUHREN

The fire crackled like a witch's laugh and its glow covered the whole room like a warm blanket. Brandy was swirled in large, bulbous glasses. The chateau's lounge was minimalistic. Wooden floor, wooden panels on the walls. The odd painting dotted here and there. The conversation dulled between the skiers I had been tutoring all day. Now was the chance I had waited for. I walked over to the fire and cleared my throat to gain the attention of the ten people or so left enjoying their après piste. They turned to me and I began. Here is the tale that I told.

***

On the 24th December 1911, three men met outside the small village of Muhren, in the Swiss Alps. Each man carried a musical instrument. Their intention was to travel to the equally small village of Gimmelwald some two kilometres away in order to entertain the older villagers with their renditions of Christmas carols. Carrying a bass drum was Tobias Niedhart. Brothers Andreas and Sebastian Gartman carried brass instruments.

They skied in silence for a while, gliding on the yielding white carpet beneath them. Andreas broke the silence, speaking to no-one in particular. "Of all the times to go to Gimmelwald you pick the one night when the cable car isn't working. Still it's only two kilometres along the freezing Verra Ferrata. So why should I complain?"

"You complain because that is all you ever do," Sebastian replied. "You complain about everything. No-one forced you to come, Andreas. Go home."

"If I went home now, I would never hear the last of it from dear mother. I would have let the family down, the village down. Those old bone-shakers down."

Sebastian held his tongue. There really was no point in arguing with Andreas. Never any satisfying outcome. With such a distance to go, Sebastian did not wish to add to the tension that hung in the air like a condemned man.

They skied side by side through the calm of the night. Tobias, who had been contemplating what to say to ease the animosity between the two Gartman brothers, spoke in a mock-jovial manner. "I hear that the folk in Gimmelwald have put on a nice spread for us. Burli, rippli and their wonderful sauerkraut."

"Oh, terrific!" said Andreas, the sarcasm in his voice very self-evident. "That makes it all worthwhile!"

"And also," continued Tobias, ignoring Andreas' barbed retort, "they have a fine selection of wine and beer, not to mention brandy and kirsch which will keep us warm for the journey back."

"Oh no," whispered Sebastian, fully aware of what was to come.

Andreas turned to Tobias. His features were as dark as the yuletide sky, as unforgiving as the mountains that surrounded them. He reached out and dragged Tobias towards him by the lapels on the drummer's coat. Tobias was a large man, nicknamed 'The Bear' in the school where he taught. He was also a peaceful and placid man. He tried to pull away from Andreas; his face had drained of colour and his eyes began to water with fear.

"The journey back. What the hell do you mean 'the journey back'?" hissed Andreas.

"Well I thought, um -" stammered Tobias.

"You didn't think, did you?" screamed Andreas, droplets of his spittle hitting the terrified face of Tobias. "It's bad enough dragging us to your stupid party in the freezing cold, never mind coming back the same night! Why didn't you arrange lodgings? I could kill you, Tobias. You moron!"

Andreas was suddenly spun around to find himself facing Sebastian, whose eyes had narrowed and whose teeth were bared and gritted. Andreas had rarely, if ever, seen his brother look so angry. It unsettled him.

"I've had enough of you, brother," said Sebastian, a moment before he sent his right fist crashing into Andreas' nose. Andreas flew backwards and came to rest in the snow with a resounding 'thwump', his skis flailing like branches twisting in a strong breeze. Sebastian stood over him and looked down with open and utter contempt.

"You deserved that," he said.

Andreas wiped his nose and flung some of his blood onto the blank canvas. He looked at Sebastian. An evil sneer spread across his lips and his eyes became hateful slits. "So, I earned that did I, Seb? Well I'll tell you something you don't know, my friend. I've been giving Fabienne something she deserves for some time now, something you obviously can't."

It took Sebastian very little time to process this information. "You've been seeing my wife? You've always been jealous of what I have. My job, my wealth, respect. So, you decided to take the one person I love above all else. You bastard!"

Sebastian hurled himself at Andreas, who was still prone. They tumbled like lovers in an eternal embrace. Fists flew, hitting and missing their targets. Words of hatred spewed forth from both brother in stark contrast with the tranquillity of their surroundings.

Tobias was unaccustomed to such displays of violence. He wanted to break up this fight. He took his drum off his back and started to hit it, manufacturing a deep, resonant sound. The two pugilists stopped their brawling and looked up at the drummer with quizzical expressions.

"I wanted you to stop and didn't know what else to do," said Tobias, sheepishly.

The two brothers looked at each other, their personal war temporarily forgotten. They started to laugh. They laughed hard and loud at the man who stopped their fight with the banging of a drum. They were still chuckling when the avalanche hit them.

The white rage sent them falling into the frozen abyss. No time to scream. No time for fear. Nothing could be heard above the dull roar of the cascading snow, not even the nauseating sounds of bones shattering against unforgiving trees or rocks that had been sleeping beneath the winter's blanket. The blood of the three unfortunate musicians that marred the terrifying beauty of this phenomenon was soon hidden by more snow. Time had lost all rhyme or reason during this awe-inspiring show of nature's might, which engulfed and purified all its path.

The landslide stopped just short of Muhren then it receded back to the mountains. It retreated in stages like a film that had been reversed. This extraordinary phenomenon was not noticed by three men who had just set out on a journey to entertain some old residents of a nearby village. Three musicians from Muhren: Tobias Niedhart and brothers, Sebastian and Andreas Gartman. The date was 24th December 1912. Once more they began their journey, their eternal journey to Gimmelwald, a destination that they would never reach.

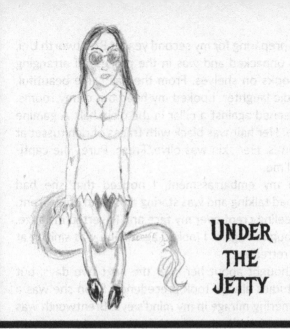

UNDER THE JETTY

Stretching out into the murky waters of the river Sten is a wooden jetty. The elements have beaten it severely over time. Its timber is grey. Large parts of it have drifted from memory. I used to drop a line into the water. Occasionally I would snare a shore crab. I would examine it, then release it back to the waves. Halcyon times.

The purpose of my return is very different. I buried something under the jetty. A long time ago. I've come back to discover if it still remains under the shingle. As the late evening sun reflects on the still waters, I dig, and reflect.

***

I was preparing for my second year at Brentworth Uni. I had unpacked and was in the process of arranging my books on shelves. From the hall came beautiful, melodic laughter. I poked my head out of my rooms. She leaned against a pillar in the main hall. A gamine figure. Her hair was black with traces of rich russet at the ends. Her skin was olive. Fresh. Pure. She captivated me.

To my embarrassment, I noticed that she had stopped talking and was staring at me. An unpleasant, hot feeling crept over my face and I averted my gaze. She laughed again. I looked again. She was smiling at me. I retreated.

I thought about her over the next two days, but my studies always took precedence. Soon she was a shimmering mirage in my mind's eye. Brentworth was a large university. I doubted that we would come into contact again.

***

A violent knock at my door had me fumbling for my glasses. The display on the digital clock shone out in the darkness, informing me of the lateness of the hour. I rushed to the door. Nobody had ever come to my rooms, except the odd bully who threatened me to write a thesis for them and arrived any time of the night or day, usually drunk or stoned. It took me a moment to focus as the hall lights flooded in. I was shocked to see *her* there.

"Hello, Samuel," she said. For a moment I thought Sophie Loren was standing there talking to me with a husky, sexy brogue. "I am so silly. I have locked myself out of my room. You seem to be a very kind man. Could I come in while I wait for the caretaker?"

"Well. Yes. Yes. Please." The words stumbled drunkenly from my mouth. She floated like a feather into my rooms. I turned the light on. She wore a silk night shirt, and the material accentuated her delicate, perfect body with every move she made.

"Would you care for a cup of tea?"

She lightly brushed my arm with her hand. "That would be perfect," she replied.

We spoke for a while. Her name was Vicky Alessi. She was originally from Sorento in Italy. She had been in England since her father had died in the Concordia disaster. Her mother sent her to Brentworth to study English as a second language along with classical art. Although I could have listened to her forever, I was aware of the time marching on. I had lectures in the morning. I was always early and well prepared for them.

"I'll go and find the caretaker," I said. "He must be around somewhere."

She stood in unison with me. I felt warm, slender fingers slip into my hand. My heart thumped furiously. My stomach flipped over several times. She led me to the bed.

"I'll be very comfortable here, with you," she whispered into my ear. She kissed me. Then she stood back. She looked at me, her smouldering, emerald eyes reaching into my mind. One by one, she undid the buttons on her blouse, her long, slender fingers never leaving the fabric between each button as they moved downwards. Blouse open, she dropped her shoulders and let the garment fall to the ground. My heart was trying to beat its way from my chest. I was fully aroused but at the same time unsure how to proceed. The moonlight formed a soft glow around her form. She sat on the bed and laid back.

"Come to me, Samuel," she said, looking deep into my eyes. I laid down next to her. She touched me. I climaxed almost instantly.

"I'm so sorry," I stammered, "I'm a virgin. Please don't tell anyone." I started to cry with shame.

"It is all right, Samuel. We will try later." She put her arm around me. I'd never felt so happy.

For the first time in my life I missed a lecture. I didn't care. Vicky and I spent the morning together in my bed. For the next few days, we had sex wherever and whenever we could. Instead of the wimp I had always been, I was now a man. I even refused the usual menacing requests to write work for others. My studies suffered. They could go hang.

We lay in bed one afternoon. We had just had sex and I was panting but I had now managed to prolong the act and satisfy Vicky. She had introduced me to cigarettes and we were smoking contentedly. Vicky raised herself up on one elbow.

"Samuel, something is wrong," she said.

I felt a heavy dullness in my heart. Was this the end?

"The head of the university has been coming on to me. Touching me. I think he wants me."

Anger rose inside me, like a burning knot of rage. No-one else should touch her. Vicky was mine. "What do you want me to do? Do you want me to beat his brains out?" I had never spoken like this before.

"No, darling," she smiled at me, "I know that the dean is a very rich man. I think we could make some money out of his desire."

"What do you mean, Vicky?"

"I will tempt him, in his office. He will try to have me. You will record what happens."

"I can't do that," I replied anxiously. "I can't let another man touch you."

"Dear Sammy," she laughed. "He will not have me. We just need to make it look like he is. Then we will ask him to consider his position at the university and his family life. He will pay."

Principal Bayliss had an open-door policy regarding his students and I took advantage of this. I positioned myself in his ensuite shower room. My mobile phone was charged and ready to record. I waited.

I heard a familiar laugh outside the office. Peering through the shower room door, I saw Vicky enter. She was quickly followed by the rotund figure of Bayliss. His face looked redder than usual and he wiped sweat off his neck and balding head. Vicky perched on the edge of the desk. She wore a short skirt and a thin, white cotton blouse. She wasn't wearing a bra.

Bayliss closed the office door.

"Lock it," said Vicky. "My problem is confidential. I do not want nosey parkers knowing my business."

Bayliss did as he was told and then went to walk to his chair behind the desk. Vicky reached out and grabbed his tie. She pulled him towards her. She wrapped her legs around his waist. She kissed him full and hard on the lips. Bayliss wrenched himself away.

"I can't do this," he spluttered. "I have a wife. I have children."

Vicky undid the buttons on her blouse. "They are not here, are they?" she said and pulled the flustered dean back to her. This time he did not move away.

I watched as Vicky had sex with Bayliss on his desk. My hands shook with rage. My stomach tied itself up into painful knots. She lied to me. Now another man had her. Despite the powerful urge to stop this gargoyle defiling my love, I recorded the whole sordid event.

Afterwards, Vicky led Bayliss out of his office and this allowed me to escape. I caught up with her near to my rooms, where I dragged her in and slammed the door.

"What the hell was that!" I shouted at her. Tears began to fall with my rage and confusion. "You said you weren't going to do that with that fat, sweaty pig."

Vicky looked at me. She smiled. Then she tilted her head back and laughed. "My little Sammy. Are you jealous, my love?" She took my hands in hers. "I did it for us. We can demand more money with what you recorded. Trust me."

I did trust her.

Bayliss received our demands with a copy of the recording. Vicky was right. He was a wealthy man. Fifty thousand pounds in used banknotes was left at a specified location. We took it back to my rooms and we made love on it. All my jealousy slipped away like a thief in the night as Vicky kissed me on the lips and then my entire body. I had money and the most beautiful woman in the world.

Vicky told me to hide the money. I wrapped it carefully and buried it. Deep. Where no-one would find it.

***

Two days after I had hid the loot, my door crashed open. I covered our naked bodies with the quilt. Bayliss stood there. He was very pale and his eyes seemed to stand out from their sockets.

"I thought I'd find you two little bastards in here," he hissed, spittle flying from his mouth in all directions.

Bayliss stared at us. He was shaking and clenching then unclenching his fists. He was ashen and I thought that he may collapse at any time. Tears weaved down his face. Tears of rage or sorrow? I couldn't tell. I could smell the alcohol on his breath. I backed away from him as I feared an immediate physical attack. Even Vicky seemed nervous as she reached behind her grasping for my hand. Bayliss stumbled a pace forward.

"My wife knows about me and you, you slut. She's left me. I have my resignation ready to tender to the university board. My life is ruined."

Bayliss spoke quietly, calmly. He was like a man who had accepted that he was going to be shot in the morning. This worried me. "Tomorrow, at nine sharp, you will give me back my money. All fifty grand of it. If you don't, then I will go to the police."

"We've spent it all," said Vicky.

"That is not my problem!" shouted Bayliss. He knocked into the door frame as he left our room.

I started to cry. Vicky held my hand. "Do not worry, Sammy darling," she said. "I have a plan."

***

It wasn't until Bayliss was opening his car door that he looked down. He stood on a large tarpaulin. He looked round. I came at him out of the lamplight. The shovel split his skull open, blood spurting out like a macabre fountain. The taste of bitter bile entered my mouth at the sound of the nauseating crack of steel on bone. He fell. I stood looking at his open, empty eyes. This was for Vicky. My love. He had violated her and the thought of that tore into my guts. I hit him again, the sound of the shovel connecting with his head sounded like someone throwing a wet towel at a wall.

"Sammy, come on," whispered Vicky. We wrapped up the bloodied dean in the tarpaulin. The grotesque contortion on his face looked like Edvard Munch's The Scream, but with added gore. This thought made me smile. He was bloody heavy, a dead weight. We placed him in the boot, and we drove off campus.

While Vicky smoked cigarettes, I buried Bayliss. Deep. Where nobody would find him.

***

Vicky gradually stopped coming to my rooms. She started to avoid me. My desire for her was still insatiable. I stopped eating. Sleep was a distant memory. I felt a heaviness in my heart, and it felt like it would break. I wished it would.

One night, I sat in bed, smoking. I stared into the gloom. Tears formed and then fell, unabated. A knock at the door. Had she returned to me?

"Yoo-hoo. Pointdexter," said a man's voice.

Followed by a familiar giggle. "I have some work for you."

The door slowly opened. One of my tormentors was kissing Vicky. They were still kissing as they entered. Vicky shut the door with her foot. When they finally parted, Vicky spoke.

"Sammy, darling. I believe you know Ricky."

"Yeah. I know this gorilla," I replied. I felt numb. I thought that I was her only one. Had she been stringing me along all this time? A tired acceptance filled my soul.

Ricky moved quickly to the bed. He grabbed my throat. I could feel fingernails piercing my windpipe. "Who you callin' a monkey, you little shit."

"Leave him," said Vicky. "We need him alive."

Ricky released his grip. He stood by my side, glaring down at me.

"I've decided that I would like that money now. All of it." The warm, silky tones of her voice when we had first met had changed into a cold, steely sound. It was difficult to believe that this was the same woman.

I tried to sound brave, confident. "What if I refuse?"

"I will tell the police that you killed Bayliss. That you forced me to help. You will go to prison for a very long time."

My head was yanked back as Ricky took hold of a chunk of my hair. "Failing that, Brains," he said, spitting all over my face, "I will rip your head off."

***

My life is a travesty now. I sleep rough. I keep moving. I keep out of trouble. I eat wherever I can. From bins behind restaurants. From the pockets of drunks. I sometimes pass by my parents' house. I don't stay long as I look out of place in this smart, suburban enclave. I walk pass posters stapled to lamp-posts. They plead for information. They want to know where I am. If I would come home. A fresh-faced, beardless me looks back at the me of today.

I killed Vicky. I stalked her for a while. I caught up with her one night as she stumbled from the uni bar. Alone. She didn't put up much of a fight as the wire tightened around her throat. Her body slumped. Blood cascaded from her neck like a multitude of red fireworks decorating the sky. I felt one more surge of lust for her. I had her, one last time.

I wrapped her body up. I buried Vicky. Deep. Where no-one would find her.

I stop digging. I lean against the jetty for a moment. Not much more shingle to move. Then I will find out. If it's still there.

THE CORNER SHOP REDEMPTION

"Good morning, Mrs Thompson."

"Good morning, Mr Cotton. Are you going to watch the cup final, this afternoon?"

"No. I'm afraid I'll be too busy in the shop. I don't even have a telly."

"Our Reg says we'll give Jerry a good hiding. Mind you, he would say that. He still hasn't forgiven them for what happened during the war."

"Well, I don't know about that. Five pence for the loaf, Mrs Thompson."

As she got to the shop door, Mrs Thompson stopped. She turned to Cotton, still standing behind the counter. "If you need help, Mr Cotton, our Mary could help. She's a good girl and she's 16 now."

"A good idea. Send her in for a chat."

***

Mary wasn't keen on the prospect of working for Cotton. "I don't like him, Mum. He's fat, sweaty and he looks at me funny," she said.

"That's no way to speak about a respected man like Mr Cotton," replied her mother. "Anyway, you've no work and no money. Now get down to that shop and take that bloody job."

Mary did not like life in the shop. Cotton would often squeeze past her. Too closely. His ample belly would touch her lithe figure, like a jellified phallus. He would creep up on her while she was stacking shelves. He would look over her shoulder. She could smell the acrid aroma of tobacco and whiskey on his breath. The wheezing sound of his breath made her freeze. The occasional drop of saliva that fell on her shirt made her nauseous.

On one occasion, Mary dropped a tin on the shop floor. She bent down to retrieve it and felt something soft and yielding on her back. Then two hands grabbed her waist and pulled her up. A wet, slimy feeling filled her ear. "You naughty, girl, damaging my stock like that. You must be punished." Mary screamed and threw her head back making a perfect connection with Cotton's mouth. He yelped and let go.

"Sorry, Mr Cotton, it was an accident," she whimpered.

Cotton had one hand under his chin, catching the free-flowing blood as it deluged from his bloodied mouth. He spat out red liquid as he shouted at Mary. "Get out, you little bitch!"

Mary ran from the shop and stopped just outside. Tears burst from her eyes. She felt as though she was in big trouble now, hitting her boss. She didn't move as an arm slithered round her shoulder like an obese python.

"There, there, my dear. Just a complete misunderstanding. Come back into the shop and we'll have a nice cup of tea and forget all about it." Cotton led Mary back into the shop, like an animal to the abattoir.

***

"I need you in this Sunday, Mary. You've been here a few weeks now. It's time for a stocktake."

"But, Mr Cotton, I can't this Sunday. I'm going..."

"I've cleared it with your mother. There'll be extra money in it for you. See you at nine o'clock sharp."

Mary found the shop unlocked. She tentatively entered the stock room at the rear of the premises.

"Hello? Mr Cotton?" she whispered. Dusty tins sat on crooked, wooden shelves. They watched Mary with indifference as she crept in.

A creak. A door shutting. Mary turned. Cotton was stood there. Sweat was running down his rotund face. The smell of scotch on his breath and clothes made Mary wretch.

"Hello, my little treasure."

Cotton slowly stepped forward. He fumbled with his belt. Mary tried to push past him. He threw her on the ground. Cotton moved forward. Mary cried out in fear. Cotton smiled. He was too big. He was too strong.

***

Mary lay on her bed. Guilt. Shame. Incomprehension. A knock on the door.

"Mary, your tea is on the table," said Mother.

"Go away!" the response.

The door opened.

"Now listen, young lady..." A mother sees her daughter. A face stained with tears. A face stained with bruises. "Mary, what happened to you?"

A cry. A release of emotion. "He touched me, Mum. Mr Cotton. He shouldn't have done it, Mum. He touched me."

***

Cotton was standing behind the counter when Mrs Thompson entered the shop.

"Good morning, Mrs Thompson. What can I get for you today?"

"Nothing, Mr Cotton. Thank you. It's about our Mary. She's in a bit of a state. She says that you touched her, you know, downstairs."

"I see," replied Cotton.

"I'm sure it's just a misunderstanding, Mr Cotton. If you could just tell me what happened."

"The truth is, Mrs Thompson, I caught Mary stealing. Money. Out of the till. She got very angry and tried to attack me. I had to restrain her."

"Our Mary? I don't believe it. She's always been a gentle child."

"It's amazing what some people will do when caught," replied Cotton. "I am quite sure that she stole money. I've checked the till. There is still some missing. Perhaps Mary has it. In her pockets or bag."

"I'll go and find out, Mr Cotton."

"Thank you, Mrs Thompson. If it's returned, I won't take any further action."

***

touched me.

Mrs Thompson found money in Mary's bag. She entered her bedroom.

"You silly little cow! Mr Cotton told me that you cut up rough when he caught you stealing. Look what I found in your bag." Mrs Thompson threw a handful of coins at Mary.

"How do you explain this?"

"I didn't do it, Mum!"

"I found the stolen money. I am so disappointed with you, Mary. I'm going out. We'll discuss this further when I get back."

***

It looked like a shop dummy. Dangling from the bannister. Mrs Thompson was mesmerised by the movement as she stood in her doorway. Swirling. Left. Right. Never ending. A moment of realisation. A scream of despair. A life lost.

Cotton had the temerity to sob almost hysterically at Mary's funeral. There was more sympathy and consolation for him than for the Thompsons. He left the wake a relieved man.

Cotton carried on. His business flourished. He employed a replica of Mary, after a suitable period of mourning. He made suggestions. He made advances. Then he made his new girl work on a Sunday. For a stock-take.

Cotton planted money from his till into the girl's bag, which was hanging on a coat hook behind the counter. He then went into the stock-room, where the girl was tentatively calling his name. He shut the stock-room door. He stumbled towards the girl. He couldn't hear her frantically pleading with him. His belt was loosened. His intention clear.

Burning icicles scorched the inside of Cottons' trousers. He was stopped dead.

"Get out. Run," spoke a rasping voice from behind him. The girl left the stock-room. The door crashed closed.

"Was she your next victim, Cotton?"

Cotton was motionless, paralysed by terror. The icicles that held him back now moved. Slowly. Down onto his buttocks. The icy heat made him cry out as the digits squeezed. He stumbled forward onto his hands and knees. He began to sob.

"Come on, Cotton. Take me again," said his assailant. "Look at me, you bastard!" Cotton turned round. There stood Mary Thompson. She was still beautiful. He could see through her white, silk blouse. Her young breasts were irresistible. He stood up. He started to shuffle, trousers around his ankles. He reached out for her.

As his fingers touched her blouse, the garment began to change. Rips appeared on the sleeves. The virgin white of the silk became a dirty, muddy brown. There was movement under the blouse. A circle of blood appeared between Mary's breasts. Cotton looked at Mary's face. Her skin was blue with cyanosis. Her head lolled almost to her shoulder. A thick rope was tight around her neck. Cotton put his hand to his mouth. It did not stifle his fearful groan as worms and maggots squirmed from Mary's empty eye sockets. He retreated. He fell.

The blood between Mary's breasts stopped spreading. There was a slight movement inside the cloth. The blouse then violently ripped open, as out sprang a large, black rat. It landed and ran towards Cotton. It leapt. Cotton let out a scream that that told of the agonising pain, the worst pain that he had ever felt, that coursed through his body. He looked down. The rat had bitten off his erect penis at the root. It scampered into a corner and began its feast.

As a bewildered Cotton, paralysed in pain and shock, watched the rodent, Mary had advanced on him. As she knelt in between his legs, Cotton turned to her. Her hand shot between his open thighs. She grabbed his blood-soaked testicles. She wrenched. She twisted. He screamed. Long and loud.

***

"Good morning," said Mrs Thompson, entering the shop. "I don't suppose you watched the football? Losing three-two to the Germans. Our Reg was furious. He still hasn't forgiven them for the war. Even if we did beat them in the final last time."

"Good morning, Mrs Thompson. No, I have no interest in football. Sixpence for the loaf, please."

"That's just like your brother. He didn't care for the game either. Still haven't heard from him?"

"No. Not for years. Anything else, Mrs Thompson?"

"No, love. You know you look very similar to him. Like you were twins. Anyway, must dash. Goodbye, Miss Cotton."

Plastic Dolls
on Lying Pages

Plastic dolls
Lying pages
She said
He said
Love you
Hate you
Who cares?

Personal tragedy
Is told in swimwear
Money famine
Where's the phone
More wealth will
Cushion the blow

Size zero
Be like me
Personal trainer
Fat to thin
Sell on disc
Return to self
Little people
Not in my gym

Perfection by
Hairbrush/airbrush
Hiding cellulite

Sell your soul
Dress yourself
In dollar bills
Leave the trash
In bargain bins

Your team
Of artists
Superficial-alize
While you smile
Through acrylic eyes
Little girls
With clear skin dreams
Hide themselves
Beyond their purse

So let us join
In avocado dip
Balsamic reduction
For the masses?
Crystal wine
For crystal hearts
Starstruck eyes
Cannot vie
White powder
Do not fear
For a ravaged nose
Makes you more.

THE PRANKSTERS

The Haversham Club, Holland Park, London, W8. A sanctuary for a certain breed of gentleman. Retired. Opulent. Enjoying the finer things in life - Montecristo cigars and Le Printemps Cognac. On the wall, in between mahogany bookcases filled with books on cricket, wine and biographies of such illuminati as Churchill and Gladstone, was oak wainscoting. This was so highly polished you could comb your hair looking at it. Hung sporadically on the wainscoting were oil paintings, copies of Titian, Caravaggio and Turner, daring any expert to expose them as frauds. Anachronistic heads of antlered stags, foxes and badgers broke up the artwork. Silence prevailed. Even loud rustling of The Times raised inevitable eyebrows. Life at the club was perfect.

One glorious August day, the tranquillity of the club was broken. Loud voices came from the atrium. The sergeant-at-arms was arguing with somebody. "Gentlemen, please. Keep your voices down. You'll disturb our members," he implored.

"Keep your hair on, grandad. Not that you've got much," replied an unfamiliar voice. Every member present turned as the lounge doors opened.

There stood the sergeant-at-arms. He was in the company of three young gentlemen. "This way, gentlemen. I will show you to your table."

The sergeant shuffled forward. The trio remained still. They all looked around the lounge. "What a dump!" said one of the three.

"It's like God's bloody waiting room," replied another.

"Here, gentlemen," said the sergeant-at-arms, desperation creeping into his voice. The group strutted over to their table. When they had settled into the high-backed red leather chairs, the sergeant said to them, "Can I take your drinks order, please?"

"Champers! The best. And make it snappy, pops," came the reply.

As he slouched away, the sergeant exchanged glances of resignation with another member.

***

Charles Penrose-Watson, heir to the Penrose property empire. Rupert Harrison-Smythe, son of The Earl of Westchester. Henry Harper-Jones, married into the Silverman stockbroking dynasty. These three ingrates had decided that the club was an ideal location to liven up their lives. If you placed these three in a line-up you could not pick them out individually. They all looked like Hitler's Aryan dream. Blue eyes, blond hair and all reaching the six feet mark. They also had an air of arrogance about them. They would not care one jot if their actions hurt or upset anyone. The attitude was that money was power and as they had the former in abundance that credo remained. With this arrogance and pseudo-power came a streak of cruelty. They played practical jokes. Some innocuous, some injurious. They offered sweets that turned the mouth blue. Next, whoopee cushions. Pranks of that ilk.

On one occasion, Harper-Jones returned to his seat to find what one would describe as fake dogs' business on his chair. He looked at Penrose-Watson and

Harrison-Smythe. They had turned red in the face. Then they started blowing bubbles. Harper-Jones picked up the fake mess and the ruse was exposed. This allowed Watson and Smythe to burst out laughing.

"Is there any decorum left in the world?" said Harper-Jones. He started to smile. Then he joined in with the puerile giggling. There was, indeed, no decorum left.

Events took a more serious turn a few days after the dog mess business. Harper-Jones and Harrison-Smythe arrived before Penrose-Watson. They placed more dog waste on Watson's seat. When he did arrive, Watson looked at his companions.

"Really, chaps. A tad more imagination required here," he said.

He picked up the waste only to discover that it wasn't fake. The other two laughed fit to burst. Penrose-Watson did not find this amusing. After a visit to the men's room, he did not return.

The club board did not find this amusing either. The three were summoned before the committee. Major Rippon, KGM, OBE, the distinguished chairman, addressed them.

"Gentlemen. Your joke-playing has now got out of hand. Consider this meeting as your final warning. Many of the committee would have you dismissed from the club at once, but procedure must be followed. However, any further disturbance and you will be expelled from the club. This might appear trivial to three wealthy young men. Let me make it clear. If you are dismissed from The Haversham Club, you will be barred from joining any other exclusive establishment in London. Many doors will be closed to you. Do you all understand?"

"Yes, sir," said the three in unison. It was a rather subdued trio that returned to their table. They vowed to continue with their pranks outside of the club.

***

A few days later, Harrison-Smythe was seen hobbling around on crutches, his right leg plastered from toe to knee. It appeared that he had made the mistake of going on vacation and entrusting the other two with access to his Kensington flat. They entered Smythe's apartment and removed some floorboards, replacing the carpet to disguise the fact. Smythe returned and fell through the missing floorboards, breaking his right ankle. Among the occasional burst of sniggering, they vowed not to carry on until their injured colleague had recovered.

One evening, after quaffing a bottle of Ardberg Galileo single malt whiskey as if it were mineral water, the three retired to a local, exclusive nightclub. Champagne was ordered and they retired to reserved seating. During the evening, Harrison-Smythe declared that he was going outside for a cigarette. Penrose-Watson announced a visit to the washroom.

This left Harper-Jones with the entourage that his wealth attracted. He didn't spend a moment thinking about his absent friends.

Later, a young woman approached Harper-Jones. She appeared to be in a frantic state.

"Are you Henry Harper-Jones?" she enquired, tremulously.

"Yes, my dear. Have some champers," he replied.

The woman leant closer to Jones and whispered. "Your friend, Rupert, is in trouble. He's in the alley at the rear of the club. I think he's been stabbed."

Jones rushed out and found his friend prone in the alleyway. A large knife protruded from his chest. Blood poured over the hand that held the knife, soaking his shirt. He beckoned Harper-Jones towards him. As Jones came close enough to hear Smythe, the latter coughed and spluttered blood over him. Smythe then rasped, "For God's sake, Henry, call the police."

After a somewhat incoherent call to the emergency services, Jones returned to Smythe.

"Go and find a doctor in the club, Henry," said Smythe.

"They told me to stay with you," responded the fraught Jones.

"You are no bloody good, Henry. I'm dying. Go and find some medical help."

Harper-Jones fled back into the club. Harrison-Smythe continued to bleed.

The police and ambulance were very quick to the scene. Harper-Jones met them where his friend had fallen. Smythe was gone. Under the wearying gaze of medics and police officers alike, Jones protested that his friend had been lying there. With a knife in his chest. Dying.

"Look. I'm covered in his blood," he exasperated.

A medic wiped his face with a gloved hand. After close inspection of the fluid from the face of Harper-Jones, the medic and a police officer came to the same conclusion. The blood was fake.

"This is the stuff that they use for actors. Film, TV, that sort of thing," said a policeman. "I think that you have had a little too much to drink and wanted to have a laugh at our expense."

"You bloody, stupid pleb! My friend is dying somewhere. Stop your arsing about and do your damn job!"

The police officer had heard enough. "Okay, you Hooray-Henry. You are under arrest for being drunk and disorderly in a public place."

Harper-Jones was then conveyed to spend an uncomfortable night in police custody.

The following morning, Harper-Jones accepted a caution for being drunk and disorderly. With tail firmly between his legs, he left police custody and wandered home to wash before attending the club.

Penrose-Watson and Harrison-Smythe were waiting for Jones. The latter's entry to the club brought forth gales of laughter. Jones stood there at the table and waited until the others had composed themselves. It took some time. Finally, wiping away a tear, Smythe spoke.

"So, Henry, old chap, how was your evening?"

More laughter. Jones was visibly shaking. His face had turned pale. His fists were clenching. He could only bring himself to say one word, "How?"

Smythe reached into his jacket and pulled out a knife. The knife had red stains on the blade. Smythe put the point of the knife to the palm of his hand, pushed the knife and the blade retracted into the handle. Jones stood there, stunned. Watson and Smythe were silent for moments before they, again, collapsed with mirth. The smile on Smythe's face lasted until Jones punched him squarely in the face. Smythe fell backwards in his chair. His flailing feet upset the table as he landed on the ground. There was no time for further violence as the club steward, a large Scottish gentleman by the name of McTavish, arranged the immediate exit of Mr Henry Harper-Jones.

It was the final straw for the board. Harper-Jones was expelled from the club. This had a quietening effect on the other two, much to everyone's relief. It appeared that all the jokes and tricks would stop.

***

The club enjoyed this return to tranquillity until a box was delivered by hand to Harrison-Smythe. Opening it, he found a short note. The letters were formed by cut out headlines from newspapers.

HERE IS A LTTLE 'PIECE' OFFERING. ENJOY.

Smythe took out a bundle from the box. He unwrapped it carefully. He screamed out loud. In the bundle was a dead rat. It smelled as if it had been floating in the sewer for a week before being wrapped up. Smythe vomited on the carcass, a sad send off for the poor rat.

Events continued to get out of hand. Harper-Jones was sat at home when he felt movement on his leg. He looked down to find a tarantula making its way upwards. It had been posted through his letterbox and eventually found its target.

Jones got into the club before it had opened on the pretence of carrying out some manual labour. Dressed in dirty overalls and a fake moustache, he applied razor blades under the table usually occupied by his old friends. The edge of the blades protruded slightly from the table. When Watson and Smythe attended later, they both suffered unpleasant cuts. Worst still, they, once again, disrupted the normal business of the club.

***

It was a few days later when each of the three received an invitation. It promised an evening of fine dining. Of free champagne. Risqué entertainment. Invitations guaranteed to appeal to the three young men.

At seven o'clock that evening, the three pranksters met at the address given on their invitations. It was an abandoned warehouse close to the dockyard. They entered tentatively. Dying lights barely lit the room, feebly illuminating broken windowpanes and cobwebs that floated in the air, like the grey hair of an old maid.

"I thought the Haversham Club was a pit," said Harper-Jones. "Who in their right mind would dine in a place like this."

"I agree, old boy," replied Penrose-Watson.

"The bloody place is falling to pieces. Look at the state of those floorboards."

"Let's get out of here and find a decent watering hole," implored Harrison-Smythe.

As they turned to leave, they heard a click. They were bathed in blinding light. A crackling sound permeated the air as an old PA system croaked to life.

"Good evening, gentlemen. Leaving so soon?"

As their eyes adjusted to the intensity of the lights' beam, the room came into focus. Situated in the centre of the bare, split floorboards stood a table. On the table were two silver candelabras. Three lit candles adorned each. Around the table were three carver chairs. At each setting was an ice-bucket containing a bottle of champagne.

"Please sit down," came the voice from the PA. "Help yourselves to the drink."

As the three took their places, each one of them activated a strategically placed whoopee cushion. They looked at each other. They smiled.

"Very amusing. Now who are you and why are we here?" said Harper-Jones.

"I am someone who understands your fondness for practical jokes. I have a joke to die for. Please pick up your napkins."

The trio did as instructed. Under each napkin was a doorbell, screwed to the tabletop. There was a thick cable running from the device, which disappeared through the floorboard below.

The PA continued.

"When you sat down each of you activated a small, explosive device. Should any of you decide to get up, the explosive will detonate."

For once in their self-indulgent lives the three had concern and fear etched into their faces.

"One of the buttons in front of you, when pressed, will deactivate the explosives. The other two, if pressed, will kill you. You have under ten minutes to decide which button is your saviour. When that time runs out, you will die. Good luck."

The information was slowly absorbed. Penrose-Watson spoke first. "This is ridiculous. There's no bombs. This is just a joke."

"If you want to stand up," said Harper-Jones, "Be my guest. If you want to gamble with all our lives, go ahead."

Penrose-Watson fell silent. He looked intently at the button in front of him.

"What the hell are we going to do now?" said Harrison-Smythe, the panic in his voice evident.

"I don't think we have a choice," Harper-Jones said, his voice barely audible. "One of us is going to have to push a button. The other two... can pray."

Sweat dripped from his nose and onto his shirt as Harper-Jones wavered a finger above his doorbell. He closed his eyes.

"Do it, Henry," hissed Harrison-Smythe.

Slowly Jones' finger fell on the button. And pressed.

They sat there. Eyes closed. Moments seemed to slip into minutes.

"We're still here," said Harper-Jones.

"You've done it, old boy," cried Penrose-Watson.

The PA buzzed into life. The three stopped their backslapping.

"Bad luck, chaps," said the voice. The voice was then replaced by a loud ticking sound. The three looked at each other. They turned in unison to an unhealthy grey tone. As smoke seeped up through the floorboard, they let out a mixture of screams and whimpers, eyes widened by their predicament. Watson rose, knocking his chair over. Watson was floored by Smythe, who then jumped over his prone friend. Before Smythe could reach the door, Jones' elbow smashed into his nose. Smythe fell, holding his bloodied nose. Jones tugged at the door.

"It's bloody locked!" he cried out. Smythe joined him. Together they tried to shoulder the door open. It remained unmoved. A loud crack made them turn in unison. In a far corner a large billow of white smoke was rising from small fire. Dust and plaster covered them as it dropped from the shaking ceiling. They could hear Watson crying as he huddled under the table.

"God, no! I don't want to die!" Smythe wet himself as the pranksters faced the end.

The shaking stopped. The smoke cleared. The door opened. In they walked. The put-upon members of The Haversham Club. They surveyed the scene. Smythe and Jones were hugging each other just inside the doorway. Watson was curled up into a ball, still under the table.

"Good evening, gentlemen. How was your evening?" said Major Rippon.

The rest of the members laughed loud and hearty. Tears were shed. Faces turned crimson. One or two members fell to the floor. Major Rippon brought back order.

"Fellow compatriots. I suggest that we re-convene at The Haversham. We must let these three young men clean themselves up. We also have tonight's entertainment to view."

Harper-Jones looked up at the Major. "You've taped all this, haven't you?" he said.

"Of course, young man," the Major sneeringly replied. "And if you do not want tonight's events openly broadcast, I suggest that you all relinquish your membership of the club. Of course, should you try and use your influential contacts then everyone on the planet will have a look at you pissing yourselves and crying like babies."

The three pranksters shuffled out like old men towards the door. As they left, a guard of honour was formed for them. A gauntlet of victory.

"I never want to see any of you again," said the Major.

The Haversham Club. A sanctuary for a certain breed of gentlemen. Retired. Opulent. And very peaceful.

George .15

THE LAST HAG

England was in chaos. The land bled and burned with civil war. From the ashes rose Matthew Hopkins, witch-finder. Using false rumours spread by the Catholic Church he raped, tortured and killed hundreds of innocent women. Harnessing the peasant's fear of the devil, stories of whom were spread by Renaissance authors, he acted undisturbed in his mission. Many women were denounced as witches. Those who took his eye in fancy found themselves in his bed. If they refused him, they found themselves tied to a burning stake. When tired of one conquest, Hopkins would find another bed-fellow before denouncing the last. As womankind suffered at the hand of Hopkins, my sisters and I hung our heads in shame. We scattered to different hiding places. And feared for our lives.

Hopkins continued his evil quest in his village of Manningtree, east of London. He claimed to have overheard a group of local women discussing their meetings with the devil. His accusations lead to their deaths. His power started. His followers grew in numbers. Old, lonely or simply hated women and girls were easy prey.

My sisters all suffered at the hands of Hopkins. All twelve of them were caught or betrayed. I felt their agony. We were all sympathetic to each other. Our thoughts and feelings were as one. Now I couldn't sense them at all. I was the last.

Driven by the desire for vengeance, I travelled to Manningtree. I settled in a small copse in view of Hopkins' house. I waited.

***

Hopkins leaves his home early to carry out his terrible business. At the midday sun, his wife leaves. Inside the house, I take what I need. Before I depart, I administered a strong sleeping potion to the marital bed.

As I had planned, this night is the first night of a full moon. My power is at its strongest during this time. I watch Hopkins ride home. As he passes, I hear the screams of his victims. A dark aura surrounds him. Blood spatters his coat. He is death. His woman, safe and untouchable, greets him. I grip the wax effigy in my hand. Soon Hopkins, very soon.

The candlelight is extinguished in the house. Under the sacred moon I begin my work. I chant the old words. I place hair taken from Hopkins' coat into the head of the doll, and I put the effigy on the small piece of cloth taken from one of his shirts. Then I carve. In the past, we used this method to kill or maim our enemies, but I have something better in mind for the Witchfinder General.

The scream pierces the morning air like the cry of a banshee. I smile as Hopkins' wife runs out of the house. She dashes to a neighbouring house and cries for help. The door opens and she goes inside. Hopkins stumbles out of his door and falls to the ground, naked. He has large, ponderous breasts. His male genitalia have disappeared to be replaced by that of a woman. His facial features are the same, only smoother. Any hair on his legs, chest or arms has been removed. I look at the finished effigy. It took me all night carving the doll into the form of a woman. Looking at the transformed Hopkins, my endeavours have been amply rewarded.

It doesn't take long for the villagers to gather and take Hopkins to the church. I mingle with the mob. No-one pays me any heed. On hallowed ground, they try to cut him, and he whimpers pitifully as his arms are targeted by many blades. This is a trick he has used many times in order to 'prove' that a woman is a witch. The knives are blunt. He does not bleed. Someone bellows, "There is no blood. Only witches do not bleed. Take her to the river." With a spring in my step, I follow the crowd.

The ducking stool. Has there ever been a fouler torture created by mankind? Hopkins is strapped into the chair. The pole attached to the seat is lowered by a fulcrum. The chair enters the river below and Hopkins is submerged. The chair is then raised after a few moments. He is still alive, so he is ducked into the water again. This is completed 13 times. Hopkins survives. He is deemed by the local clergy to be cursed. The crowd roars.

Watching Hopkins tied to the stake in the village square, I begin to feel guilt. I have seen this horror too many times. Some of my sisters died this way and I felt the agony of the flames as they perished. Hopkins has the nerve to cry for mercy. He still keeps the form of a woman. The form I created. I cannot bear this. While the flames lick around his legs, eager to advance, I move to the back of the crowd and take out the wax doll. I begin to carve.

This time I sever the breasts on the effigy. A crude representation of the male sexual organs are fashioned next. The mob gasps in unison. My work on the doll has transformed Hopkins. He has become a man again. The fire devours the cowardly murderer in his true form. The guilt lifts from me. I enjoy the rest of the show.

DINNER AT THE MILLERS'

"**A**re we gonna do this or not?"

I looked across the table at Buck. He leaned back in his chair, feet up on the table. He was taking sips of his whiskey like he didn't have a care in the world.

"I don't know, Buck," I said. "Seems pretty strange."

"Billy, Pa always said you shoulda been born a girl. If you don't wanna help, I'll do it myself."

I drained my red eye. "Tell me again what you saw, Buck."

"I was in the town store before I met you in the saloon. This couple came in. They were dressed real fancy. The woman had a pretty dress on. The man had a suit with tails. I saw a gold watch chain in his waistcoat. They went up to the counter and put a list down. The old fella serving looked at the list. His eyes widened. Billy, I swear that ol' shopkeeper stacked enough food and shit to keep the whole union army goin'. The man, he checked the goods and then pulled out wad of dollar bills as thick as a rifle butt. There was some talk 'bout delivery and then the two fancy dans left. I went up to the storeman and gave him some bull about the woman bein' my old schoolteacher and that I sure would like to catch up with her for old time's sake. He bought it and gave me the directions to their place. Written here, Billy. You can read them, can't you?"

I looked at Buck's eager face. Having money to spend during the winter sounded good. It was better than hauling logs for sale around Oregon. "Let's do it, Buck," I said.

It was hard going through the snow. Jessie didn't like pulling the sleigh. The snowfall had made the logs heavier. Jessie snorted and whinnied, and often stopped. Me and Buck would have to pull on her reins to get her moving again. The place that we were headed for was two miles north out of town. It was on the edge of Sun Pass Forest, which Buck and I knew well. Time dragged along with our journey. Then Buck shouted, "Look, Billy. Smoke risin'. This has to be the place."

We stopped some distance from the house.

"We need a plan, Buck," I said. "If they're home, we'll ask them if we could come in out of the cold. Try to sell them some logs. If we get in, then I'll bring out the shotgun. If not, I'll give them the shotgun at the door. Either way, we're leavin' rich."

***

The house was huge. I counted eight windows in the front. That included the large window that opened onto the upstairs balcony. Buck started knocking on the door.

The door opened and a woman came out. "Yes? Can I help you?"

"Sorry to bother you, ma'am," I replied. "My brother and I are sellin' logs for winter fuel. Would you care for any?"

The woman was dressed in a silk blouse. Her skirt was a deep, blue velvet and her underskirts were a shining white. From her face, it appeared that she had not slept for some time. Her colour was ash. Red lines ran from her bloodshot eyes.

"I'll speak to my husband," she said. As she went inside, I turned to Buck.

"Is that the woman from the store?" I whispered.

"That's her," he replied.

We turned back to the door. There stood a man. His face was adorned by a large moustache which had grown across his cheeks. Despite this mass of facial hair, I could see that he had the same grey/red colouring as the woman.

"What do you want?" he said. He looked sideways at Billy and Buck with well-founded suspicion.

"We were jus' sellin' logs, sir," said Buck.

The man turned to the woman. "Martha, we were in town this morning ordering logs. Have you forgotten?"

"I remember, Charles," she replied. "But we are getting low on other supplies."

Charles looked back at us. He grinned. "Boys, where are my manners? I'm Charles Miller and this here is my wife, Martha. Come in out of the cold. Let's get you a tot of whiskey."

The inside of the house was full of furniture. Chairs and tables with designs and patterns on them that I had never seen before. There was a big, white piano with lit candles on it. A granddaddy clock chimed the hour in the corner.

"Here we are, boys," said Charles, offering us glasses of whiskey. "Can you look in the cellar first, see how many logs we might need for the furnace down there."

We walked down into the basement, carrying a candle each. Charles followed us holding his own candle. We paused at the last step. "Mister," I said. "There ain't no furnace down here."

"You're damn right there, boys," said Charles. We looked at him. He was pointing a Colt pistol at us. "You both throw your coats and boots over here," he said.

We did as we were told. Martha came down to the cellar and collected our clothes. Feeling my coat, she found something else. "Well now," she said, pulling out my shotgun from a large pocket inside my coat. "And what were you going to do with this?"

"Martha, it appears that our guests were thinking of robbing us," said Charles. "Why else would they bring a gun into our house?"

Charles and Martha left the basement. The door shut. The key turned.

Our candles were still alive. We looked around the cellar. You couldn't fit a horse and wagon inside it. This could be why there was nothing in here. Cobwebs and dust, but no furniture or supplies. What were they going to do with us?

"*Jeesus!*" cried Buck.

I looked at him. He was looking at the floor. Under the dim candlelight, I saw a pair of hands grabbing Buck's leg. Then a pale face. A torso wearing a union army uniform. No legs, just dirty, bloody bandages wrapped around rounded stumps without much care.

"Help me, please," said the man, grabbing Buck's leg.

"Who are you? What the hell happened?" I said, dragging the man to rest against a wall.

"I'm Vic McCabe. Me and a friend was goin' home after fightin' Johnny Reb. We was tired an' hungry. My friend, Ike, was hurt. He could barely walk. The two upstairs picked us up in their wagon. They promised us food an' drink. When we got here, they forced us at gunpoint into the cellar." The man wiped away some tears and continued. "Ike was taken upstairs. I heard him screamin'. When he was brought back into the cellar he was missin' a leg. After a while they took him again. They took another leg. The next time they took him, he didn't come back. Then they started to take me."

The man pointed to where his legs used to be. "Next time will be the last time."

Buck pulled me to one side, away from Vic. "What the hell is goin' on, Billy? Why they takin' bits of body?" He was shaking, his eyes as wide as supper plates.

"We gotta get out of here, Buck," I replied, "there's somethin' ain't right here."

"What, Billy, what is it?" I looked at Buck.

"I think the Millers might be eatin' people." Buck backed away from me.

"That's not true," said Buck. "It can't be true." Buck ran up the stairs to the door. He started banging on that door like the Dogs of Hell were chasing him.

"Let me out, you sons of bitches," he cried out. "Open this Goddam door!"

It wasn't long before Buck ran out of gas and leaned against the door. He started sobbing. The door opened. Buck didn't fall through it because Charles Miller held him up.

"Shut up, you cowardly bastard," he said. Then he pushed Buck down the stairs.

I rushed over to where Buck had landed. I relit his candle with a match to take a good look at my brother. He was bleeding from a cut on his head. A couple of his fingers were bent out of shape. A lot of blood was coming from his left leg. Something was poking through his jeans. I touched it. Buck yelled out in pain. It was his shin bone.

"Jesus, Buck. It's a goddam bone stickin' out of your leg. It's sticking out of your fuckin' leg."

***

There was no means to measure the time. The Millers came and took Vic. He hollered. He tried to fight them. He lost. Buck was laying with his head on my lap, mumbling to himself. Now and again he would scream. I stroked his hair and his brow. Sweat oozed out of him. I was so thirsty that I licked some of Buck's sweat from my fingers. The door opened. I tensed up. When my eyes had become used to the light, I saw Charles standing in front of me.

"It's time," he said. He had the Colt pointing at me.

"I ain't goin' nowhere with you," I replied, my voice shaking.

Charles cocked his pistol. "You'll come. If not, say goodbye to your friend there."

I looked at Buck. Chances were that he was going to die without being shot. He had lost a lot of blood. I wasn't going to take that chance.

Charles took me up to the kitchen. Martha was there, holding a meat cleaver. "Get on the table," she said. I laid on a big, wooden table. I gulped hard. The table was covered in dark stains. They tied me with thick, leather straps. Martha stood by the side of my legs. She raised the cleaver. I stared at her in disbelief. I couldn't believe what was happening.

"Martha," said Charles. "Why don't we start with an arm this time. Just for a change."

Martha came up the table. She raised the cleaver. There was a thud of metal biting into wood. I passed into welcome darkness.

***

I woke up in the cellar. The pain struck me immediately as I looked at the stump that used to be my left arm. The wound had been bandaged, and no blood was seeping through. I ripped off some of my shirt. I struck a match against the brick wall and set fire to the cloth. I looked for Buck. He was lying on his front, his face touching the cold stone.

"Buck! Buck! Wake up."

Buck had a terrible smell about him. I looked at Buck's injured leg. I pulled his jeans away. Buck's leg was dark. Not just around his broken bone, the dark flesh had spread all over his leg. I moved him carefully onto his back. His skin was clammy to touch. Buck had stopped breathing.

I sat against the wall and rocked back and forth. I cried for a while, then got angry. I began to punch the basement wall with my one arm. When this became too painful, I started kicking out. I screamed in anger until my throat felt like I had swallowed hot coals. The Millers had killed Buck and I wanted justice for my brother. I needed a weapon. Feeling along the wall I found a loose brick. Easing it free, I crawled over to Buck.

"I'm sorry, Buck," I said as I brought the brick down hard onto Bucks chest. I heard bones cracking. I raised the brick again.

The key turned in the lock. The door swung outwards from the cellar. There was the shape of Charles Miller against the bright background. I lurched forward and plunged my weapon into Charles' neck. He staggered backward. Sticking out from Charles Miller was one of Buck's rib bones that I'd snapped out of my brother's chest. I had sharpened the end against the floor. And now I had stabbed this bastard with it.

"You all right, Charles?" said Martha as she approached us. I picked up the Colt pistol that Charles had dropped. Martha saw me. She then looked at her husband writhing on the floor.

"You little bastard!" she cried, and hurled towards me. Without hesitation, I shot her. A patch of red seeped through her blouse. She looked back at me. She was smiling. I shot her again, the bullet smashing through her skull. She slumped to the ground.

I sat in the parlour for a while. I helped myself to some of The Millers' brandy. I was trying to make sense of what had happened. I needed to get the law. They wouldn't know that we were going to rob the Millers. I stood up to go. Standing by the door to the hallway were three children. The two boys were dressed in suit jackets and shorts. The girl had a floral dress. They stared at me with bloodshot eyes which peered out from their grey faces.

"All right, kids," I said without confidence. "I'm just gonna leave now. I'll bring back some help for your ma an' pa."

As I edged towards the door, one of the boys hissed at me. Then all three rushed me. I yelled as one of the hildren bit into my calf. I was bigger and stronger than these kids, but it was difficult fighting as I was dog-tired, not thinking straight and only had one arm. I picked up the girl and threw her across the room. She smashed into the piano and lay still. The boys were trying to bite me. I pushed one away and this gave me room to strike the boy. I punched him in the face. He fell to the ground. The other boy stopped to look at the boy on the ground. I took this chance. I kicked him, hard, in the groin. He cried out and bent over double. I ran out of the house.

I returned to the Millers' house with a sheriff and a couple of deputies. They saw the blood-stained kitchen table. They found my arm. They brought Buck up from the cellar. One thing they didn't find were the Millers. Charles, Martha, the children. They were all gone.

No More Heavenly Deals

We scoured the solar system. Peace, Plenty, Panacea and me. From the furnace of Mercury, through the rings of Saturn, to the edge of beyond. There was no sign of her. We settled above Earth. We took stock.

"Why has she left, Life?" said a forlorn Peace to me.

I pointed to the blue orb below. "She has lost faith, Peace," I replied. "She wanted a perfect world. She did not get it."

"What are we to do, Life?" asked Plenty.

I thought for a moment. "We have choices, my brothers. We can stay and fight War, Pestilence, Famine and Death. We could stand up for mankind until the evil discovers that she has gone. Then we flee. We could leave the Milky Way and find her. She would not abandon us completely. She would leave a trail." I paused. "Finally, we could take flight immediately. And leave man to his fate."

Peace was the first to speak. "I say leave now. Man has been fighting each other from the moment he knew how. It is War that creates Famine and Pestilence. War will never end on this planet. Mankind is always developing new weapons, new ways of destroying each other. They are doomed."

"We should battle on," replied Plenty. "During the most bitter conflicts there has still been food. With the advancement of their sciences, mankind has progressed in providing sustenance. They have genetically modified crops. They will soon be able to create synthetic foodstuffs. They will not starve."

"I agree with Plenty," said Panacea. "Man has made significant leaps in the area of medicine. New antidotes and nursing methods continue to be discovered. We must stay for now. I can nurture their understanding. They will survive."

They turned to me. They waited for my decision. "If there was a chance that we could suppress War. If we could reduce the amount of fighting. Then Plenty and Panacea might be able to persuade man to direct his efforts. He could be swayed to be more constructive. Instead of destructive. What do you say, Peace?"

"We could try, Life. We will need one more ingredient thrown into the mixture," replied Peace.

"Settled," I said. "We stay."

Panacea, Plenty and Peace left me for their daily struggle against the Evils. I prepared for my later meeting with Death. Would Death harness War? Would he give man the opportunity to change?

"Life!" shouted a voice. I looked up. Peace was flying towards me at speed. "She has taken it. We are lost."

"What has gone, Peace?" I replied.

"We arrived at the table with the map of Earth. It was on the floor. The chest, with Hope inside, has vanished."

Hope was the ingredient that Peace had mentioned. Without Hope in the hearts and minds of man, our endeavours were pointless. She kept it in the chest under the table where good and evil battled for Earth's soul. I never thought that she would flee with it.

I arrived at the table with Peace. War, Famine and Pestilence had taken their positions. Plenty and Panacea gave me a fearful look.

"What have you done with the box?" I asked.

War spoke, "We haven't touched your box. Life. Let us start proceedings."

I looked at Peace, Plenty and Panacea. "It's time to go," I said. As one we flew into the eternal void. We left Earth to its fate. I took one last look back. The Evils were rushing towards Earth. It was theirs now.

We travelled through the loneliness of endless space. I feared that we would never find Her. A comet approached. I've seen so many, but still its beauty held me in thrall. The ageless rock and ice enveloped us. We tasted its aroma, and it was something familiar. We followed as it passed.

The comet took us to the edge of beyond. It slowed. It stopped. It transformed. It was Her.

She looked tired. "I have tried hard to forget, but I can't let go. Life, return to Earth. I have to know what has become of man."

The Evils had been busy. Those not fighting in the numerous wars that ravaged the lands were suffering beyond human tolerance. Orchards and crops had been burnt to destruction. Animals lay rotting on the scorched earth, caught in the crossfire of man's rage. Warships rampaged across the oceans. In their wake lay fish in the dirty water, dying.

Weakened by hunger and bereft of medical supplies, kept for the plethora of armies, man succumbed to all diseases. Wasted cadavers of lost souls. Untouched. Unloved.

I found War. He was revelling in the destruction. Gloating at the carnage. I whispered into his mind. "You've done well, my friend. Now it is time for the grand finale. Your crowning moment. Finish it."

War turned around, grinning at thin air. He then disappeared.

I didn't stay to see codes being entered or buttons being pressed. I heard the collective scream of humanity. A tear zig-zagged down and fell onto my robe as the clouds of death rose.

I don't know if she will create again. She's still tired and heart-broken. If she does then Peace, Plenty, Panacea and I will stand with her.

We will do better next time.

CPSIA information can be obtained
at www.ICGtesting.com
Printed in the USA
LVHW032359290920
667478LV00008B/1022